"While I was in here, I stumbled on this."

Grady stepped away. "It's one of Mr. Edison's talking machines. However, I think you're all going to be surprised at the recording."

"Oh, just shut up and crank the blasted thing. Maguire!" grumbled Carlisle.

Grady looked at Maggie and rolled his eyes, and then began to turn the crank. There was a second or two of static, and then a man's voice, made tinny and thin by the instrument.

"Sorry about the boat, but you see, I couldn't allow you to leave the island. And really, it was much nicer than blowing it up, which is what would have happened had you caught the captain in time. I wonder, should I tell you who I am? It might be more amusing if you don't know. But no, I'll take pity on you. By Wednesday, when the boat comes again, you'll all have been killed by your old friend Sam Warden. I'm right here, among you. I'll be seeing you all, seeing you all, one last time."

Don't miss the first book in this thrilling new series

Murder at Bent Elbow

MORE MYSTERIES FROM THE BERKLEY PUBLISHING GROUP . . .

SISTER FREVISSE MYSTERIES: Medieval mystery in the tradition of Ellis Peters . . .

by Margaret Frazer

THE NOVICE'S TALE
THE OUTLAW'S TALE
THE PRIORESS' TALE
THE SERVANT'S TALE
THE BISHOP'S TALE
THE MAIDEN'S TALE
THE BOY'S TALE
THE MURDERER'S TALE

PENNYFOOT HOTEL MYSTERIES: In Edwardian England, death takes a seaside holiday . . .

by Kate Kingsbury

ROOM WITH A CLUE
SERVICE FOR TWO
CHECK-OUT TIME
DEATH WITH RESERVATIONS
DO NOT DISTURB
EAT, DRINK, AND BE BURIED
GROUNDS FOR MURDER
PAY THE PIPER
CHIVALRY IS DEAD
RING FOR TOMB SERVICE

GLYNIS TRYON MYSTERIES: The highly acclaimed series set in the early days of the women's rights movement . . . "Historically accurate and telling."—Sara Paretsky

by Miriam Grace Monfredo

SENECA FALLS INHERITANCE
BLACKWATER SPIRITS
NORTH STAR CONSPIRACY
THROUGH A GOLD EAGLE
THE STALKING-HORSE

MARK TWAIN MYSTERIES: "Adventurous . . . Replete with genuine tall tales from the great man himself."—*Mostly Murder*

by Peter J. Heck

DEATH ON THE MISSISSIPPI
A CONNECTICUT YANKEE IN CRIMINAL COURT
THE PRINCE AND THE PROSECUTOR

MAGGIE MAGUIRE MYSTERIES: A thrilling new series . . .

by Kate Bryan

MURDER AT BENT ELBOW
A RECORD OF DEATH

A RECORD OF DEATH

KATE BRYAN

BERKLEY PRIME CRIME, NEW YORK

A RECORD OF DEATH

A Berkley Prime Crime Book / published by arrangement with the author

PRINTING HISTORY
Berkley Prime Crime edition / August 1998

For information address: The Berkley Publishing Group, a member of Penguin Putnam Inc., 200 Madison Avenue, New York, NY 10016.

The Penguin Putnam Inc. World Wide Web site address is http://www.penguinputnam.com

ISBN: 0-425-16537-X

Berkley Prime Crime Books are published by The Berkley Publishing Group, a member of Penguin Putnam Inc., 200 Madison Avenue, New York, NY 10016

PRINTED IN THE UNITED STATES OF AMERICA

10 9 8 7 6 5 4 3 2 1

A Record of Death

Prologue

Mid-August, 1883
Wiggstree, Washington

The man paused in the darkness outside Mrs. Hatcher's Post Office and Notions. It was two in the morning, and everything was closed. The dirt streets were dark and vacant, illuminated only by moonlight. Shutters were drawn. Even the dogs were dead to the world.

He reached into his coat and pulled out a stack of envelopes. They were thick, the paper being ivory vellum and very expensive, and they contained several enclosures. He had them almost in the drop slot, but at the last moment, pulled back his hand to spread them like a deck of cards in the moonlight.

Mercury Marchand, Rance Carlisle, Mr. and Mrs. Roman Kellogg, A. M. Andrews, Gus Thorpe, Phoebe Perch and the Maguires were the addressees. All correct. Three years of plotting, planning, and research were represented at this moment by a handful of stamped, neatly addressed envelopes. He straightened the stack again and smiled.

Each and every one was an invitation: an irresistable invitation from someone each addressee couldn't possibly turn down. Of course, the alleged hosts had no idea they'd asked their friends to a gathering.

The top envelope was addressed to Maggie Maguire's detective agency in San Francisco, and the woman it was ostensibly from, Lolo Carré, was in reality away on an extended tour of Europe. With Maggie, he'd appealed with friendship. This Lolo Carré was an old friend, a dear friend, from Maggie's carnival days. Never underestimate the power of research.

For the others, he'd used different tactics. Vanity, the promise of an illicit weekend, nostalgia, whatever it took.

They'd come, that was the important thing. They'd come, like moths to a lamp, like metal filings to a magnet. Like pigeons to the roost.

"Get on with it, Warden," he muttered under his breath, turning abruptly and shoving the envelopes through the slot in the door. "There's still work to do."

He had logs to chop, he thought as he turned and walked down the deserted street. Ropes to buy. A fish to catch. A snake to feed. By the time his lovely pigeons arrived, everything would be ready.

Everything.

ONE

TWO WEEKS LATER
SAN FRANCISCO

"JUST ONE MINUTE, *LIEBCHEN*."

It seemed that all conversations with Otto Obermeyer were sporadically interrupted by "just one minute"—or, more often, "*nur eine minute, bitte*"—and then a dive under the couch. This one was no different.

Seated at her desk, Maggie Maguire regarded his backside as, on his knees—and a hand and a shoulder—Otto groped blindly underneath the sofa. At last, giving a triumphant cry of "Ha!" he lifted his shaggy, white head, and held up a small red rubber ball.

A Siamese mix—all round face and short plushy coat and enormous blue eyes, with a body color that had darkened from barely watermarked-and-white to distinctly striped-and-white over the last few years—regarded the ball philosophically from the back of the sofa. He twitched an ear.

Peering at Maggie over his half-glasses as if there had been no pause in the conversation, as if he was not in a totally ridiculous position for a grown man, Otto said, "So, what you waiting for? This woman, she makes the invitation, you should go. A long time it has been since you had an evacuate." He threw Ozzie's ball and got up dusting his knees.

"A vacation," said Maggie softly, and turned to stare out the window. She leaned back at her desk, picking up the letter opener, which, after a moment, she flung thoughtfully at the side wall. It stuck. Having no more blades at hand to fling, she toyed with the envelope that was the source of contention.

Behind her, Otto clicked his tongue. "Vacation, then. Grady gonna be mad, you put the holes in his paneling again."

She didn't reply. She always put holes in the paneling. And Grady was always mad.

He always fixed it, though.

Outside, water streaked down the huge, multipaned, semicircular window in the loft that served as office to M. Maguire & Co., and a haze of vapor clung to the inside. Another damp and rainy afternoon in San Francisco. Well, at least the rain pushed the fog out of the way for a little while.

Still gazing out the window—or trying to—she said, "I really want to go, Otto. Except, I wonder if Grady's up to it. The invitation's for two, and besides, it's not like I can just run off and leave him alone when he's like this." She swiveled her chair toward the old toymaker. "He's got me worried."

Otto leaned back on the couch, running a gnarled hand over the leather. "He just bin all knotted up over that little flibbertigibbet Cosgrove girl," he said. "He gonna get another one pretty soon, forget all about her. You wait and see." He glanced toward the floor, an indulgent look on his face. "Oh, Ozzie. Again, you put?"

Slowly, he got down on his knees again and peeredn under the couch while the cat sat calmly by, waiting for his toy. Head under the sofa, voice muffled, Otto said, "So, Lola-somebody invites you to this island. Who is she again?"

Maggie tipped the card out of the envelope again. "It's Cutthroat Island. And it's Lolo, not Lola. Lolo Carré. You've heard me speak of her?"

"The walker on the tightrope?"

"No."

"The ballerina mit ponies? Or the lady trainer of elephants?"

Maggie smiled. "No. The Fabulous Flame Dancer. She jumped a flaming skip-rope and twirled fiery batons. Like that."

Otto raised his head, lips pursed, then said, "Your papa, he had many interesting actors." He threw the ball, a red streak, for Ozzie.

"Acts," she said, absently.

"Acts, actors: same thing, about." He heaved himself up onto the sofa again. "So what wants this dancer mit the batons on fire? A party? Maybe you go fishing on this island?"

Maggie studied the paper again, brows knitting. "A reunion, I guess. There's just a card that says, 'Your presence is cordially requested at the Wapiti Lodge, Cutthroat Island, Washington, on September five through twelve, as guests of Miss Lolo Carré.' "

For the umpteenth time, she turned the card over, searching for Lolo's oddly neat, foreign handwriting. She already knew that it wasn't there. Odd that the invitation didn't have a personal message, but then, Lolo had been having trouble with her hands. Arthritis. It was why she'd retired. Well, marrying all that money hadn't hurt, either—Chicago stockyards, really big money—and then *boom*, her husband dropped dead. Lolo had written that she was a widow practically before she tossed the bouquet.

Maggie ran her thumb over the engraved letters, the thick ivory vellum stock—it was a fancy invitation. Lolo was too sensitive about her hands, that was all. She hadn't wanted to mar it with what she must consider an arthritic scrawl.

She looked up and said, "That's all there is. No R.S.V.P., just be there. Otto? Ozzie can get that himself, you know."

Oho was on the floor again, this time retrieving the cat's ball from beneath a chair. "*Ja, ja,* I know. But I don't . . . *eine minute, bitte* . . . there," he said, and again lobbed the ball across the polished floor, the oriental rugs. The cat gave an acrobatic leap to one side and galloped after it. Otto rose again, smiling, and settled back on the couch. "So. And you want Grady should go with you?"

"I think it would do him a world of good, don't you?" she said. Mostly, she thought, it would provide a change of scenery. Maybe he'd meet another pretty young social climber, maybe an heiress, or even a waitress. Maybe several, of all shapes and sizes, which would be best. Grady, her cousin and business partner, needed a distraction. And she couldn't imagine anything he'd find more pleasantly distracting than a flock of pretty women to charm.

Ever since Miriam Cosgrove had dumped him he'd been dragging around the office like an opiated tree sloth. Just "Yes, Maggie" or "No, Maggie" or "Use a coaster, Maggie." Never spoke a word unless he was spoken to first. And even then, he said as little as possible.

He'd even asked her—twice—to answer the telephone. His sacred telephone, his pride and joy!

And he hadn't taken apart anything mechanical in over two weeks. Normally she'd expect to find some new whatsit torn to pieces and spread out over the client table about once every ten days or so: screws to the left, nuts and bolts to the right, everything else in some sort of order only Grady and Otto—his partner in mechanical disembowelment—understood.

But he'd bought that Edison two weeks past and he had yet to play one of the cylinders, let alone begin the dissection process. It just wasn't like him.

She looked up to find Otto studying her.

"This Lulu woman," he said. "She is good friend to you, yes?"

"Lolo," Maggie corrected again, with a smile. "And yes, she is. She left the carnival when I was fourteen, but she always wrote me, even after Papa died. She still writes. She's retired now, lives outside Chicago."

She fingered the invitation. "I'd really like to see her.

It'd be fun! We could rehash some old times, catch up on the gossip. . . . After all,'' she said, justifying to herself—again—the time away from the office, ''we don't have any cases pending right at the moment. Not urgent ones, anyhow. God knows Grady's been pouring himself into work lately. We're practically caught up. And it's not like it'll cost anything. She sent tickets.''

She held them up. Two train tickets, two tickets for the coach ride from the train station to the docks, and two tickets for the boat which would take them to Cutthroat Island and the Wapiti Lodge.

Ozymandias watched the ball roll beneath the couch again, slowly blinked his cornflower blue eyes, then jumped up onto Otto's lap. Otto scratched the top of his head and, eyes slitted, the cat began to purr loudly.

Working blunt fingers between two furry ears, Otto said, ''Then you better make to go. I talk to Grady for you. And—*Ach, schnitzel*! Stop making mit the toenails!'' He moved the cat's feet to a less strategic location, where Ozzie resumed kneading, and looked up at Maggie again. ''You leave it to Otto, *liebchen*. I come up mit something crafty. You see, Otto make everything hinky-dinky.''

''Hunky-dory,'' Maggie said, and then, quite suddenly, she grinned. ''You just want to get your hands on that Edison, Otto. Don't think I don't see you staring at it every time you come upstairs. You're practically salivating to rip it apart, aren't you?''

He shrugged. ''Well, maybe I got a superior motive.''

Still grinning, Maggie said, ''Ulterior.''

He shrugged again, and a smile tickled the corner of his mouth. ''*Ja*,'' he said, ''I suppose I got that, too.''

Two

"KIDNAPPING, THAT'S WHAT IT WAS," GRADY grumped. "You shanghaied me, you and Otto." He sat across from her, arms folded defiantly, as the coach clipped along the coastal road. "The damn cat was probably in on it, too."

"You're being silly," Maggie said lightly. "Ozzie had nothing to do with it." She caught another glimpse of ocean through the pine and spruce before it winked out again, obscured by trunks and undergrowth. The road was relatively smooth, and if Grady would just stop complaining, she probably would have been having a good time.

"False pretenses," Grady said. "I could sue, you know." He stared out the window. Not the shore window, which would have given a view. No, out of sheer persnicketiness, he looked out the landward window. Rocks. Tree trunks. Weeds. Ferns.

Maggie sighed. "Grady," she said, "I'm only going to apologize to you one more time. I'm sorry we told you there was an urgent case. I'm sorry we told you it was life or death. I'm *especially* sorry Otto made up that story about Mr. Edison having been kidnapped and hauled across country and held for ransom by Russian traders with big furry hats. All right?"

Grady slid a glance her way. "He never said anything about big furry hats. I would have known you for a couple of frauds right off the mark if anyone had mentioned big furry hats. But no. It was rush, rush, rush, and no conversation, and for God's sake don't answer any of Grady's questions."

He tugged the glasses off his nose and set to polishing them. "I'm really annoyed, Magdalena. I should be in San Francisco, getting the Higgenbottom paperwork together. I should be filing the insurance report on that Conklin matter. I should be . . . well, I just shouldn't be here, that's all. There are all sorts of pressing matters that need my attention."

He put his glasses back on, gripping his arm and putting on his most long-suffering look. He'd been shot on a case a few months ago, and even though his arm had long since healed, he still clutched it when he was feeling especially put upon. The trouble was that he could never remember which arm it had been, and so grabbed a bicep, left or right, however the mood took him.

But at least he was talking to her, she thought, and that was a decided step forward. He hadn't said a word on the train, except for "Excuse me" and "Pass the butter." Thank God she'd brought a couple of dime romance novels, and had been able to lose herself in *Love's Breathless Murmur*.

Grady had just sat there, moping and staring out the shivering glass, and all because she'd broken the news that there was no Mr. Edison, no kidnapped genius, no glorious adventure to save the torchbearer of the new age of invention. Grady'd stayed on the train, though. Of course, she was beginning to think he was only sticking around to punish her, when all the time she was trying to cheer him up.

She opened her mouth, thinking to tell him that there'd be other girls—really, she'd had no idea he was so serious about Miriam Cosgrove—but then thought better of it. Best not to mention the girl at all.

Besides, they were coming to the landing.

The coach broke through the final screen of poplar, pine,

and beech to stop before a neatly kept log building—the only structure they'd seen since they'd passed through the little town of Wiggstree.

"Good gravy!" breathed Maggie as she stepped, with a soft crunch, onto the gravel drive. The little building and its view of the ocean were absolutely charming. Pink and red impatiens bloomed in the window boxes, cushioned by bright displays of coleus. There were lush beds of ferns, then bluebells, along the landward side of the building, and a small placard over the door read WAPITI LODGE—EMBARKATION POINT—WELCOME GUESTS in brass letters.

Leaving Grady to grump and grumble over the bags, Maggie walked down the slope to the cabin—not that anything so nice could be called a mere cabin, really, but she didn't have another word for it—and stepped onto the decking.

It jutted firmly out over the water, held up by thick pilings. At the end of the deck, a stairway led down a few feet to the large floating dock. Moored to this was a sailboat, perhaps forty feet or better, freshly painted, with the words *Wapiti Princess* crisply lettered on the prow. Three men in white uniforms were working on the boat's deck, hauling luggage about. The cove must drop off rather steeply for them to get the boat so close to shore, she thought.

She leaned over the rail, and one of the men, a big, lean fellow with a tidy mustache and a tattoo, looked up and smiled. "Going to the island then, Miss?" he called.

"Yes, I am." It was a gorgeous boat, all white paint and shiny brass fittings and neat coils of rope. The sailor wasn't unattractive, either. Wapiti Lodge was looking better and better.

He glanced upshore, toward the coach. "You the Maguires? Party of two?"

Maggie nodded, and he said, "We'll get those bags for you then, Miss Maguire. You can wait in the dock house, with the others."

Others? Had Lolo invited other people, too? Maybe it was to be an entire party! There'd be nothing to shake Grady out of his doldrums like a flock of circus people. Well, either that, she thought with a sudden smile, or they'd send him screaming for the hills.

"Yes," she called down to him, grinning out of all proportion. "Yes, thank you!"

She turned, and nearly ran headlong into Grady, who was burdened by three grips, an umbrella, and two hatboxes. He dropped them where he stood. "I should have known," he said indignantly, still on the subject of Edison and false pretenses. "I should have known it wasn't true when I saw what you were packing. Hats!"

She put her hands firmly on his shoulders and looked him in the eye. An angle, granted, but it was doable. "Grady," she said, "get over it. Just be glad that Mr. Edison, wherever he is, is alive and well and inventing his brains out so that you and Otto can have more gadgets to take apart."

She dropped her hands to his upper arms (picking off a stray Ozzie hair along the way), and said, more gently, "Leave the bags here. The men from the boat'll get them." She looked past him, at the coach driver, who was bringing the second load. "Now, stop pouting and come inside. We're here to have fun, remember? And you won't have to ride any horses, I promise."

He shook his head. "You know, sometimes you are repulsively cheerful." And then, face filled with pious forbearance, he took her arm and stoically led her over the cabin's threshold.

"Well, how-do, folks! Looks like we got us some more company," said the rather weathered and distinguished (and decidedly portly) man who stepped forward. His skin was deeply tanned, his thick hair and closely cropped beard were nearly the color of silver, and he was dressed in the fashion of a Western businessman, from the neatly creased hat to the double-yoked suit, right down to the fancy walking boots.

Grady stuck out his hand, momentarily too astounded to be peevish. "Grady Maguire, at your service, sir."

The man took it and gave it a hearty shake. "Ransom Carlisle, out of Cutback, Wyoming. Call me Rance. Cattle's the trade, Circle C beef. That's my little homestead. 'When you eat meat, think Circle C,' I like to say. We make a profit on everything but the *moo*." He dropped Grady's hand and swept up Maggie's, kissing the knuckles. "And who might this sweet prairie bloom be?"

Much to Grady's surprise, Maggie didn't fling him out the window. She actually blushed—blushed!—and said, "Maggie Maguire, Mr. Carlisle. Charmed to make your acquaintance."

Carlisle pulled himself up and said, "Now, don't tell me you two are married! Why, it'd break my heart!"

Grady did his best to appear bored and said, "Never fear, Mr. Carlisle. We're just cousins. You have a clear shot at her."

Maggie gave Grady a daggered look, to which Carlisle was oblivious. "Call me Rance, son," he said again. "Just Rance is fine, or just Carlisle. Can't abide a 'Mister.' " He tucked Maggie's hand through his arm, and turned toward the rest of the waiting party, which, aside from an apronned serving girl, consisted of only two others. Grady followed.

"Allow me to introduce Mrs. Perch," Carlisle said, indicating the young woman, small and dark-haired and exquisitely dressed, who sat in the corner, gloved fingers curled delicately around a teacup.

"Phoebe Perch," she said, and her voice was like honey and bells. Mr. Perch was nowhere in sight, and Grady thought he was falling in love. Then she scowled. "Have those miserable wretches loaded the boat yet? This is taking forever."

Grady gave a little grunt. He hoped Phoebe Perch and Rance "Everything but the Moo" Carlisle weren't indicative of the rest of the guests. While Maggie was muttering her hellos to Phoebe, he turned his attention to their final companion, who stood up and offered his hand.

"Augustus Thorpe, Mr. Maguire," he said. He was short, with his sandy hair cut in a bristle brush, and looked as though he'd just stepped off the back of a bucking bronco. He was distinctly out of place. Grady liked him immediately. "I'd admire it," continued Augustus softly, "if you'd call me Gus."

"Gus it is, then," said Grady. "And please, don't be so formal. Call me Grady."

"You got a deal," Gus replied, then swept off his hat and offered his hand to Maggie, who was just coming up, still stuck to Rance Carlisle's arm. "Ma'am? Augustus Thorpe. Call me Gus."

"Charmed," said Maggie. Grady noted she made a point of not looking his way. He supposed he'd been a little dreary, but didn't he have a right? Here he was, all set to rescue the century's greatest inventor—probably the greatest inventor of the next century, too. And then to discover—all right, be told—it had been a hoax!

There was no need for it, no need at all. He would have come along if she'd just asked. Well, no, he supposed he wouldn't. He would have stayed home and moped over Miriam.

He sighed. Miriam. Beautiful Miriam. Blond Miriam. Soft, pink, dimpled Miriam. To think she'd eloped in the middle of the night with some common actor she'd only known four days! Why, it made a fellow's blood run cold! Her poor mother was mourning like she'd been eaten by alligators, and her father refused to speak her name.

It was a scandal, pure and simple, but far more importantly than that, it was a slap at Grady's manhood. The nerve of the girl! The unmitigated gall! To run off with an actor—a character actor at that, and not even, by God, a leading man!—when she could have run off with a fine catch like Grady Maguire.

Not that he would have considered eloping with her, of course; not in a million years. Why, he wasn't the marrying kind, not with the likes of Miriam, anyway, the wretched little wench.

Damn.

And Edison. Why did Maggie and Otto have to bring Edison into it? And why did Maggie have to be in such a blasted good mood?

"Grady?" Maggie was tugging at his coat. "Grady, come on!"

He scowled at her, just on principle, and followed the others outside and down the staircase. The dock rose and fell gently beneath his feet, and he had the first mild wave of what promised to be a lovely case of seasickness. He couldn't see the island from the shore. Wonderful. Just splendid. Off in the distance, farther than he could see, Lolo Carré was probably torching a chicken coop, all to welcome Maggie and her soon-to-be-green cousin.

"Grady!" Maggie again. Why didn't she just toss him off the dock and hold his head under and get it over with?

"Coming," he said, and walked up the gangplank to join the others. He was barely seated when the men cast off and the boat slid clear of the dock.

Rance Carlisle, a man for whom Grady had already, in the space of seven minutes, developed a deep and abiding loathing, had cornered Phoebe Perch in the back of the boat. Aft? Was that what you called it? He was probably regaling her with glamorous tales of meat packing on the open plains.

Little Gus Thorpe was in the front—The bow? The stern? The forecastle?—talking to one of the sailors.

Maggie sat with her arm through his, along the side of the boat—he couldn't remember what you called it, but it was the left side, anyway. She was gazing absently at the back of Rance Carlisle's head.

Maggie said, "I thought there'd be circus people. Oh, well. Maybe when we get to the island."

He said, "How can you stand that awful windbag?"

She turned toward him, smiling. "Carlisle? Oh, pish. We'll only be here a week. So what if he's a windbag—he's colorful! He told me he was invited by these old friends of his for high states poker. They have a game every year, in a different place each time."

She stopped, studying his face. He knew his expression was strained, but Maggie apparently interpreted it as stubbornness, not a queasy stomach. "Good Lord, Grady," she said, "this is our vacation. Relax and have a good time!"

On the sound of her last word, he bolted for the rail in a fit of nausea, and remained there, more or less, for the entirety of the voyage.

THREE

THEY HAD BEEN AT SEA FOR LESS THAN FIVE MINUTES when Maggie first made out the island peeping over the horizon. Being possessed of excellent sea legs, she walked to the front of the boat (pausing at the rail to give Grady a comforting pat on the shoulder), and sank down on a long bench. Chin propped on one hand, the salt air filling her lungs in a most agreeable way, she gazed out over the rolling blue water and watched Cutthroat Island growing steadily larger.

"Some sight, ain't it, Miss?"

Gus Thorpe, one hand clamped atop his hat, had come to stand beside her. She indicated the stretch of vacant bench. "Sit down, Mr. Thorpe. The boat makes quite a breeze, doesn't it?"

He sat. "It sure does. I been fightin' the goshdarned wind for my hat ever since we left the dock. And it's Gus, ma'am. Every time I hear 'Mr. Thorpe,' I think somebody's talkin' to my daddy."

Maggie smiled. There were certain names that, while fitting an adult, she couldn't imagine attached to a child. Gus was one of those names. "Have you been here before? I mean, is it your first trip to the Wapiti Lodge?"

The cowboy leaned toward her slightly, his face dead serious—and a little frightened, too, if she didn't miss her guess. "Oh, it sure is, ma'am. I ain't never been out of New Mexico since I was eight or nine."

Maggie wasn't surprised. Gus appeared to be in his mid-thirties, weathered before his time. He looked to be a career cowhand, one of those fellows who could spin his horse on a bottle stopper while he rolled himself a smoke and sang a lullaby to the steers, but who was at a social loss with anything higher up on the evolutionary scale than a Mexican bull.

She said, "You'll pardon my asking, Gus, but you don't seem like the type to . . . Well, what in heaven's name are you doing so far from home?"

"Been askin' myself that, ma'am." Taking the rail in a death grip with one hand, the cowboy put his head down into the wind—to hold his hat on, Maggie supposed—and dug a hand into his pocket. "See, my old buddy—Smiley Dowd's his name—he asked me out here."

He lowered his voice, though no one was near them, and confided, "Him and me, we're workin' on a cattle deal. A real big one. He paid up front for the whole shebang, and I couldn't hardly say no, could I? Wouldn't have been polite-like." He unfolded an envelope and handed it to her, then clamped his hand down hard on his head again. "See? I brought it in case they was fixin' not to let me in. I heard this outfit was real high tone."

She opened the flap and tugged out an invitation. Except for the names of invitor and invitee, it was an exact duplicate of the one she'd received from Lolo. Well, perhaps the hotel had sent them, being full service and all. Hers had been postmarked at Wiggstree. His had been, too, she noted as she stuck it back in its envelope.

"You reckon these sailor-boys know what they're doin'?" Gus continued nervously. She handed the invitation back. "All this water," he went on. "It's just so . . . wet. Ain't hardly natural, if you're askin' me."

She laughed, couldn't help herself, really, and when he looked stricken, she quickly said, "I'm sorry, Gus. It must look strange to you, coming from the desert and all."

"Ain't all deserts," he said, a little defensively. "Up in the high country, it's—"

"Everything all right with you folks?"

It was the sailor, the one with the tattoo, and Maggie found herself beaming at him like an idiot. She started to fight it, then reminded herself that she was on vacation, dammit. Quincy certainly hadn't made *her* any commitments yet. Besides, he was back in San Francisco tied to his desk. She was here, and it was all right to have a good time. And if that good time included ogling sailors, then, by jingo, ogle she would.

Augustus appeared a tad put out by the interruption, but she smiled up at the sailor and said, "Everything's splendid, thank you, just splendid. Will it be much longer? Before we reach the island, I mean. How soon will I be able to see the hotel?"

"About twenty, twenty-five minutes, Miss Maguire," he replied. "Wind's come up a bit since we set to sea. But you won't see the lodge from the water. It's inland about a half mile. Would you care for a complimentary refreshment? Irish coffee? Champagne? We have several liqueurs, also Earl Grey tea, brandy—"

Maggie held up a hand. "Oh, by all means, champagne!" She looked back at Grady, who was still hunched over the rail, and holding on for dear life. "I'll have Mr. Maguire's too," she added brightly.

The sailor turned to Gus, who was staring out over the water, the invitation clutched in his fist. "And for you, sir?"

"You got any bourbon?"

"Yes sir, we have a fully stocked liquor cabinet. Would you like that neat, or with soda? We have ice."

Gus was still watching the water. "I thought I saw . . . Are there big fish out there?"

"Yes sir," the sailor said. Maggie took the opportunity

to sneak a glance at the seat of his trousers, which were on her eye level. She blushed.

"Like whales? And sharks?" asked Gus, his voice breaking.

"A few," said the sailor, never changing expression, ever pleasant. "They have a special beach for swimming at the lodge, sir. It's roped off with metal shark nets, and nothing can get through. Perfectly safe. Now, how would you like that bourbon?"

"Double," said Gus. He had broken out in a light sweat, despite the breeze. "And straight, without no water anywhere near it, which is how I'm fixing to be as soon as possible."

Maggie stood in the bow, drinking in the scenery, as the *Wapiti Princess* slid up to the end of the long dock and was tethered alongside it. The island was lush and green and thickly wooded, at least this part of it. She still couldn't see the lodge, but the grounds coming down to the dock were well-manicured, and there was a large sign on the shore, near the dock, that read, WELCOME TO CUTTHROAT ISLAND, HOME OF THE WAPITI LODGE. On one side of the letters an artist had painted an elk. On the other side was an eye-patched pirate flashing a sword. Beyond, and bordered by two broad sweeps of lawn, a gravel lane snaked back into the trees.

The air was balmy, nothing like she'd expected. When she remarked on it, one of the sailors, a short and dark man, told her it was because of the tropical currents sweeping up from the Sandwich Islands.

"There's a trail, Miss," he said, shouldering a trunk: Phoebe Perch's, by the look of it. "The Tropical Isle Trail. Real pretty over on the other side. Got a big sand beach an' lots of flowers, even this late in the year."

The trunk he was carrying was white with brass trim and a tiny pinstripe of coral, and matched the other hatboxes and handcases piled on deck. Yes, definitely Pheobe's. By comparison, Maggie's luggage—what there was of it—looked shabby, as if she'd just gone through the house grabbing random, mismatched cases willy-nilly. Which, of course, she had. Not that any of them would have matched anyway, she thought with a sigh.

Well, Phoebe Perch could keep her matched luggage. She could keep her sordid past, too. Oh, she'd heard all about Phoebe. It hadn't been all that many years ago that she'd turned up, out of nowhere, to charm railroad magnate Thelonius Perch out of his socks—and probably a few other undergarments, too. She had also charmed him out of his considerable fortune, for the old fool had married her—and conveniently died within two weeks, under rather mysterious circumstances. Something about his slipping in the bathtub.

The whole town buzzed with it for several days. Not long after, Phoebe sold the family mansion and moved to Sacramento. Rumor had it that, socially, she kept herself, well, rather busy.

To be polite about it.

Did Phoebe plan a clandestine meeting with her beau of the moment? If so, he must already be on the island. She'd shown no interest in Gus Thorpe (who was making his way up the dock, keeping to dead center), and she'd grown bored with Rance Carlisle's tales of Wyoming winters after three minutes, turning her back on him rather rudely, so Carlisle was out of the question. Frankly, Maggie couldn't wait to see this lover. Or, if they were keeping it a secret (which they probably were), to figure out who he was.

Ah, well. This was a vacation. There was plenty of time to puzzle out the little mystery of Phoebe Perch's beau. In the meantime, the whole of Cutthroat Island and the fabulous Wapiti Lodge lay before her. Or would, once she could see it through the trees.

She bent to Grady, who was decidedly green around the gills. Poor thing. He didn't travel well, except in trains or cabs. "We're here," she said, putting her arm around him and trying to keep from smiling.

"I know that," he growled, weakly. "Just help me off this damned dingy."

"Now, now," she cooed, walking him down the gangway, trailing the others. "Don't be beastly."

When they set their feet on the shore, Rance Carlisle was busily taking one of the sailors to task. "Well, where the hell is it?" he thundered. "If you think I'm *walking*, you've got another thing coming, Long John Silver. I'm Circle C beef, dammit, and people who know what's good for them don't treat me this way."

The sailor—Maggie's sailor—stood calmly. "My name isn't Long John Silver, sir. And I'm certain the coach will be down any minute now."

His feet on dry land again, Grady had recovered sufficiently to ask, "Is there a problem?"

Phoebe Perch turned toward him and said, "You could say that. You most certainly could say that." Her thin, dark brows were knitted together, and there was a decidedly unhappy twist to her mouth. "There's no coach. No coach to take us to the inn or the lodge or whatever it is. What are we supposed to do? Walk through the wilderness in this heat? And I don't know what they expect us to do with our luggage. Really, this is most annoying."

Grady muttered, "Sorry I asked," and inwardly, Maggie groaned. Phoebe was the sort of woman who got her back up in the worst possible manner. Wouldn't go three feet out of her way to help herself, saw everyone else on the planet as her servant, and couldn't do a damned thing except complain about how put-upon she was.

Gus pushed back his hat and said, "Miz Perch, ma'am? I might could take a lope up the path, there, and see what's holdin' them folks up. Maybe they busted a wheel or somethin'."

"No," said Maggie, smiling not at Gus, but very sweetly at Phoebe Perch. "Why don't we *all* take a walk? It's hardly wilderness,'' she added quickly, when Phoebe opened her mouth. ''And it's not that hot. Just Indian summer, that's all. We can leave our things here, and—'' She turned toward the tattooed sailor, who looked a lot bigger now that they were on land. ''Excuse me sir, but what was your name?''

''Billings, Miss. Captain Billings.'' Was it her imagination, or did he wink?

''Yes. I, uh . . . yes.'' She felt heat creeping up her neck. Drat it! ''Captain Billings can send a wagon down later for the bags,'' she said quickly, turning away. ''I'm sure it's just a simple mix-up.''

To the sounds of Phoebe Perch's complaints, as well as those of Rance Carlisle, the party started up the little lane, through the trees.

''Such charming company,'' Grady said lightly, running his handkerchief over the back of his neck. ''Delightful conversation, a boat trip, no Edison . . . I just want you to know, Maggie, I'm having a lovely time.''

She slapped at a bug, and her hand came away bloody. ''Oh, be quiet,'' she said, and marched on, shoes crunching the moist gravel.

FOUR

ONE MINUTE THEY WERE TRUDGING UNDER A CANopy of pine and Douglas fir, and the next, they had gone round a bend in the lane and the lodge lay before them. It was skirted all around with gently rolling green lawns and landscaped tennis and badminton and croquet courts. Farther down, on the south shore, was a stretch of white beach. The sand had been set out with big umbrellas and chaise longues, and a large horseshoe-shaped cove served as a swimming area. Maggie squinted, and saw the buoys that marked the netted barrier bobbing gently in the blue water. A lone, lanky man stood on the shore, legs set wide, arms crossed. He didn't notice them, but looked, instead, out to sea.

The lodge itself was immense and purposefully rustic. Two stories high and rambling, it was constructed of logs and smacked of solidity. Color filled the flower beds: pink and red and white petunias, bluebells, Queen Anne's lace, and some kind of bright orange flower she'd never seen before. A white Angora cat was stretched out on the lawn, taking a sunbath.

Any trepidations Maggie might have felt brewing melted away at the sight of the Wapiti's broad verandas and porches. Deep in shade, they were set about with brightly patterned, thick-cushioned chairs, and just waiting for her to sink down into one of them, put her feet up, order a lime fizz, and catch up on old times with Lolo.

"It's perfect," she whispered to Grady as the party trooped up the lawn, toward the lodge.

"Not bad," Grady allowed, eyeing the tennis courts.

Captain Billings had loped ahead of them, and by the time they climbed the front steps, he was coming out. He did not look pleased. "Jerry, you and Rob run back to the stable and harness a team," he barked to the crew, who had trudged up behind them.

Then he softened his face for the guests. "Sorry," he said. "I can't seem to turn up Mr. Carson or Mrs. Friar." He brightened somewhat artificially, and added, "I'm sure everything will be fine. Why don't you folks go on in and have a seat in the lobby? We'll have your bags up here in no time."

He tipped his hat, and disappeared around the side of the lodge.

"I've got to say," said Carlisle, "it's a shoddy way to run a business. Why, if I ran the Circle C like they run this place—"

"Oh, do shut up about that filthy ranch," Phoebe Perch snapped, walking past him. "I've only had your acquaintance an hour, and I'm already sick to death of the damned place." She strode into the lodge, her nose in the air.

"I . . . well, I . . . By God, madam!" Carlisle huffed.

Maggie patted his arm. "There, there, Mr. Carlisle. The trip made her cranky, that's all."

Grady piped up, "I know it did me." He folded Maggie's hand into his left arm, then swept his right toward the door. "Shall we, Miss Maguire?"

They entered the Wapiti Lodge, Gus Thorpe trailing in their wake like a puppy, Rance Carlisle remaining outside with his umbrage.

The lobby was cool and shadowy, and filled with all manner of comforting furniture. Straight away, Maggie slipped free of Grady's arm and sank into an upholstered chair. It might as well have been a womb, for the way it fitted her.

She closed her eyes, smiling. "Let me die now," she murmured contentedly. Then louder, to Grady, "Has Lolo checked in yet?" She picked up a brochure and languidly fanned her neck with it.

There was a *ding*, then *ding ding ding*. Rance Carlisle, it seemed, had made his way into the lobby and to the front desk, and had apparently located the bell. He banged it a few more times, and when that failed to produce any results, he stalked off.

Maggie held the brochure before her. "This is interesting," she said. "And I quote: 'When the first American traders landed at beautiful Cutthroat Island in seventeen ninety-three, they found plentiful elk (called by the Indians *wapiti,* thus the Wapiti Lodge). They also found bear and deer, small game, and evidence that they were not the first white men to come here. Speculating that the island had been a stopping place for pirates, they further guessed that the pirates had left a fabulous cache of gold and jewels. Twenty years of searching later, treasure seekers failed to find anything more valuable than the original cave with its crudely carved utensils. However, the island has retained the name of Cutthroat Island, in memory of those—' "

"Really, dear," broke in Phoebe Perch, ennui dripping from every word. "Must you read aloud?"

"I think it's real interestin', ma'am," offered Gus. "I mean, about them pirates and all."

"You would," sniffed Phoebe.

Grady rolled his eyes.

"Excuse me?" They all looked toward the stairs, where there stood a medium-sized man of indeterminate age, dressed in tweed. He looked, in fact, to have made every attempt to come off like an English country squire.

"At last!" thundered Carlisle, striding toward the stair. "I suggest you explain yourself, sir. We've been waiting at least a half hour—"

"Five minutes," Grady interjected.

Rance shot Grady a look that said it was a good thing they weren't in Wyoming, by God, and continued, "A half hour. Where have you been? There was no coach to collect us."

"We had to walk from the beach," said Phoebe.

"I didn't mind s'much," said Gus.

"Oh dear! Oh dear, oh dear!" said the man on the stairs. "I'm afraid there's been a misunderstanding. You see—"

"I should say so," said Phoebe.

"No, no," he said, coming down the stairs, although Maggie wondered how he had the courage. "I don't work here. No, not at all! You see, when we checked in this morning—well, we weren't exactly checked in. That is, we checked in ourselves, if you get my meaning, just sort of picked our own rooms . . . Well, I thought perhaps Mr. Weintrout was with you."

Grady stepped forward. "When *we* checked in?"

Phoebe brightened. "We get to pick our own rooms?"

Rance thundered, "Who's this Weintrout fella? Just what in tarnation is going on here?"

"Stop!" said Maggie. She was on her feet now, and the lobby grew silent. "Honestly. If you'll all just calm down? This is supposed to be a vacation spot. Now everybody . . . just . . . *relax*!" The last, she said through gritted teeth. Lolo couldn't arrive soon enough to suit her. To the new man, who had descended to the foot of the stairs, she said, "Might we know your name, sir?"

"Andrews, madam," he said, obviously glad for a sane voice. "A. M. Andrews, from Portland, Oregon. I was hoping Mr. Weintrout was among your party. I was supposed to meet him here—we're going elk hunting, you see—and if he's not coming until tomorrow, that's another day I'll have to wait. Elk hunting's best in the early morning."

Next to her, Gus opened his mouth, but Maggie held up her hand, silencing him. "You said 'we?' Were there more in your party, Mr. Andrews?"

"Yes, certainly. Well, not in my party, exactly. But they came over with me on the boat. There are the Kelloggs." He lowered his voice, and said, "They write those trashy books. Those Westerns. You know, the ones by Roamin' Rex Roman?"

"Anyone else?"

"Me, I guess." The voice came from the front entrance to the hotel, where a lean, athletic-looking man in his mid-fifties—the one Maggie had seen standing on the beach—was just coming in the door. He wore loose-fitting clothes, sweat-stained, and had a towel slung over his neck.

He stuck out his hand to Grady, who was closest, and said, "Marchand's the name. Morris Marchand."

Grady immediately straightened. "Not *the* Morris Marchand? Morris 'Mercury' Marchand? The world's fastest man?"

Well. Grady was going to have a good vacation, after all, Maggie thought smugly. Give him somebody famous to tag along after, and he was happy. Although she'd be damned if she knew who Mercury Marchand was.

Marchand grinned, obviously flattered to be recognized. "Well, I used to be the fastest west of the Mississippi, anyhow, in my younger days. Don't run anymore, except for myself, just to keep in shape. Got a tailoring business now, down to Tombstone. That's in the Arizona Territory. And you'd be . . . ?"

Grady colored and quickly said, "Do forgive me! Grady Maguire, at your service, sir. May I present my cousin, Maggie?"

Introductions were made all around, received with greater or lesser enthusiasm, and then Mercury said, "Why don't you folks go get your rooms staked out? They're expecting a real big crowd. Might's well get the spot you like."

Mr. Andrews ran up the stairs ahead of them, defensively protecting his door from claim jumpers. Mercury showed them down the hall.

"I'm in number twelve," Mercury said, "and the Kelloggs have got seventeen. Only saw her on the boat over. She had a headache. Anyway, after that I guess it's up for grabs until somebody tells us different."

Phoebe marched up the corridor, opening doors then slamming them.

Augustus Thorpe went to the door next to Mercury's, opened it, said, "This'll do me fine!" and went inside, a big grin plastered over his face.

Rance Carlisle took off in the opposite direction from Phoebe.

"I could pick easier if I knew where the convenience was located," Maggie whispered to Grady—or intended to. He was already off, poking his way down the hall.

Mercury tipped his head toward her. "Pardon me for overhearing, Miss, but this place has got 'em in every room, just about. There are some that share, and some with private, uh, baths." He stood straight again and smiled. "Bet you the Queen of England herself doesn't have it so good."

Maggie grinned back. She liked this Mercury—she would have liked him fine even without the land speed records. She was about to reply to him when Grady called to her from down the hall. She excused herself and went.

Grady pulled Maggie around the corner of a hall intersection, and said, "I've got your room. Well, mine, too. They're perfect!" Bowing, he opened the last door at the end of the hall. " Madam. Your chamber. Mine's across the hall, and I staked out the one next to you for Lolo."

Maggie clasped her hands together. "Oh, Grady!" she said, delighted. "It *is* perfect!" What was perfect, too, was that Grady seemed to have come out of his funk. For the moment, anyway.

Now that they were alone, Grady had begun babbling all about Mercury Marchand, reciting times and distances and records off the top of his head.

While all of his obscure trivia washed over her, Maggie crossed the thick carpets, past a full length-mirror and a tall four-poster bed, and went to the window. There, she parted lace curtains to find a sweeping view of the sporting courts and, below them, the swimming cove.

On the front lawn, Captain Billings was arguing with an older woman, dressed completely in black. For a moment, it gave her a start—the woman could have been Miss Sophia Beckmeyer, the old biddy who ran the academy where Maggie spent her last two years in school.

"—and then he disappeared from sight," Grady finished. "Absolutely astounding to find him here, of all places!"

"That's nice," Maggie said absently, squinting to make absolutely certain it wasn't Miss Beckmeyer.

"Mags, did you hear a word I said?"

"What? No. Sorry, Grady." She laid fingers over her lips and tapped. "Either Mrs. Kellogg has finally emerged from her room—and if she has, she's awfully drab for a writer of potboilers—or Captain Billings has dug us up some staff."

Grady came and looked over her shoulder. "Well, a staff member, anyhow."

FIVE

GRADY BEAT MAGGIE DOWNSTAIRS, BUT EVEN WITH all their rushing, Captain Billings was no longer anywhere in sight. Their luggage was, however, and so was the woman in black. She stood in the open doorway, arms folded, in silhouette against the afternoon sky.

Grady stopped abruptly at the bottom of the steps—mainly to avoid falling over Phoebe Perch's trunk—and Maggie ran into him with an *oof* and a bubble of laughter that was cut short.

"There's been a mistake," said the woman in black.

"That's obvious," said Maggie, from behind him. "I take it you're not Mrs. Kellogg?"

At last the woman moved out of the doorway and to the interior, where Grady could see her face. She was about forty-five or fifty, he guessed, and as unfortunate-looking a woman as he had ever seen. And since he came from the Barbary Coast with its cribs full of woofers, that said quite a bit.

The woman was sallow complected and thin, with no discernable cheekbones. Close-set eyes and a minimal chin had made a dismal marriage with a receding hairline. Grady would have sworn that had he pitched her face-first into the desktop, she would have stuck, nose-first, like an axe. He even heard Maggie give a little gasp of shock at her first sight of the woman's face.

"No," the woman said, through lips so thin they were hardly there at all, "I'm not Mrs. Kellogg, whoever she is. I'm Mrs. Friar. And you people will have to leave."

"Leave?" said Grady. "We just got here!" The last thing he wanted was another boat ride, especially so soon in the wake of the last one. He suddenly found himself desperately wanting to stay, if only for a day or two.

Maggie ducked under his arm, took the last two risers and stepped forward, swinging one-handed over the trunk and then digging into her ever-present handbag. She produced the invitation from Lolo Carré and held it out. "I think the mistake is yours, Mrs. Friar. Obviously, there's been a mix-up of some sort. I expect Miss Carré on the next boat."

Nice bluff, thought Grady. Actually, they had expected Lolo to be there to meet them. It was really quite odd.

Mrs. Friar, who seemed unaffected by Maggie's little display of acrobatics, handed the paper back to her. "I've never heard of this Miss Carré, and there won't be another boat. The lodge is closed all this week and the next. You'll have to leave."

"My dear Mrs. Friar," said Grady, using his most soothing and—he hoped—appealing tone. He stepped down off the stairs at last. "If there's been a mistake, it's not been ours, I assure you." Unlike his cousin, he climbed over the trunk. "There are quite a few of us." He navigated his way through a pile of bags. Drat that Maggie, anyway. She always made everything look so easy! "Why on earth would the boat have come to pick us up if you were closed?"

"That's right," Maggie said. "They even had a list of our names. At least, the captain knew who I was. He called me by name."

Mrs. Friar's brow furrowed—at least, it did on the right side. The left side seemed to be frozen in place. She suddenly strode across the lobby, marching just slightly out of step around the luggage to the front desk, and it dawned on Grady why her face was so oddly unanimated, and why she walked off-kilter.

Into Maggie's ear, he whispered, "She's had a stroke."

Maggie nodded.

"I can still hear just fine, young man," Mrs. Friar announced with a glare. And then she said, "See for yourself about the reservations. I'll show you the book."

They followed, facing her across the counter, and without looking at it, she spun the reservation book toward them and opened it with a flourish. "You see? No reservations until the week after next."

"Mr. and Mrs. Roman Kellogg," Maggie read aloud. "Mr. Morris 'Mercury' Marchand. Mr. Grady Maguire and Miss Magdalena Maguire. Mr.—"

"Let me see that!" Mrs. Friar twirled the book back around and stared at it for a moment, the color draining from her face. "This . . . this is impossible! These weren't here!"

"When was the last time you looked?" asked Grady.

"This morning," she said softly, "before I went down to clean the bunkhouses. I don't even recognize the handwriting." She looked up again. "But this won't do! We got no chefs, no maids, no guides, no lifeguards, no tennis coach."

"No one?" asked Maggie.

"Not even a busboy! They all left for the mainland two days ago."

"With Captain Billings?" asked Maggie.

"No, no, Captain Swope was on that day. He had to make six trips." Her gaze fell to the list again, Grady and Maggie read along with her, upside down. All the names were written in the same formal hand. At last Mrs. Friar said, "Are *all* these people here?"

Grady said, "Afraid so."

"Afraid of what?" It was Rance Carlisle, coming down the stairs. "You finally find somebody in charge, Maguire?"

"Depends on how you look at it," said Grady, not smiling.

Mrs. Friar slammed the reservations book shut. "Well, you'll just have to leave, that's all there is to it. I haven't the resources to take care of nine people! Someone will have to run down to the landing and stop Captain Billings before he leaves."

Grady crossed his arms. "Don't look at me. My feet hurt already."

Maggie scowled. "Grady! Mr. Carlisle can't go," she scolded. "He's too old and fat to run."

Carlisle, who had managed to navigate the luggage unscathed, pulled himself up indignantly. "Miss Maguire! I'll have you know I can still bulldog a steer just fine if I have to. I'll go. I can't wait to get off this rock. Nobody t' tell me which room is mine. Bags piled all over creation. No maid to bring me towels or turn down my bunk after I finally pick out a spread for myself. And no room service. I'm hungry, dammit! This just plain wouldn't happen at the Circle C!"

Grady opened his mouth, but Carlisle barked, "Shut up, Maguire! I've have enough of your smart-mouth sass. We'd by Christ shoot you in Wyoming for a Nancy-boy!" He turned to Mrs. Friar for the first time, stammered at the sight of her, then turned to Maggie. "None of my poker buddies are here," he resumed, "and I'm beginnin' to think somebody's played a joke on me. Well, nobody plays a joke on Rance Carlisle! I'll get those fellas back up here if I have to swim out to get 'em."

With that, he stormed out the door and began to lumber toward the path through the wood.

"Somebody ought to tell him not to swim," said Mrs. Friar, softly.

"Nancy-boy, eh?" said Grady, leaning an elbow on the desk. "You'll forgive him, Mrs. Friar. I don't suppose he can help being a star-spangled ass. And don't tell me to go after him, Mags. I hope he steps in a bear trap."

Maggie patted his arm. "There, there. Don't worry about that Nancy-boy business. I hear that in certain parts of Wyoming they shoot anybody who bathes."

"What's going on down there?"

Grady glanced up to see Mr. Andrews peering down at them from the top of the stairs. Grady ignored him, as did everyone else.

"Well, Grady," continued Maggie, "I wouldn't *dream* of asking you to run down the hill after Mr. Carlisle." She was just a little too wise about it, if you asked him, but he was in a generous mood what with Carlisle being gone and all. He let it pass.

"Good," he said. "Wise decision."

"So go upstairs and get Mercury."

"Brilliant!" Grady said, standing up. "Mercury! Obviously the man for the job." He started for the stairs.

"Hello? What's going on?" called Mr. Andrews again.

"Half a second, Andrews, and I'll explain everything," said Grady, once again crawling over the bags on his way to the stairs.

SIX

GRADY, SLOUCHED AGAINST THE HOTEL'S ENTRANCE and paring an apple, looked down the front lawn and announced, "Here they come." As he turned to go inside, he passed Maggie and whispered, "You're not going to be happy. Serves you right for that Edison thing." She made a face at him and went to the door.

Grady was right. She wasn't happy. Mercury and Carlisle were coming up the lawn alone, and Mercury was assisting Carlisle, who was moving slowly and was obviously in distress. Mercury saw her and held up a hand, palm-up, as if to say, "Oops."

"Well?" asked Mr. Andrews, from behind her, and she turned to look at him. He hadn't bothered to get up from his chair. Instead, he sat stroking his mustache and close-cropped beard, and affecting the look of bored aristocracy—or at least his version of it. Studiously, he flicked a bit of dust from the leather elbow patch on his jacket. "Are they coming back or not?"

"Yes and no," she said. "They're coming back, but only Mr. Carlisle and Mr. Marchand."

That got Andrews on his feet. A little theatrically, he asked, "But what about the captain? What about the boat?"

"I reckon we can make the best of it," offered Gus, sitting on the stairs, arms on his knees. "Somebody ought to get started on supper, though. My stomach's settin' in to growl. I missed my lunch."

"Leave it to you to think about food at a time like this, you illiterate cowhand!" snapped Phoebe. "How long am I going to be stuck on this miserable island with the likes of you?" She looked at the others. "And you and you and you!" She spun and wound up, quite accidently, facing Mrs. Friar. Phoebe paled then quickly said, "And this hideous thing! I could just strangle you all!"

With that, Phoebe gathered her skirts and stalked up the stairs. As one and in silence, they watched her. Grady was the first to speak.

"Mrs. Friar tells me the next boat doesn't come until Wednesday?"

Mrs. Friar nodded.

"And it's Sunday," he continued. "Three and a half days." He cocked his head toward the staircase leading to the second floor, where they could hear the receding echoes of Phoebe's sharp steps. "With that."

Gus said, "Aw, I bet she ain't so bad, once you get to know her."

Dryly, Maggie said, "That's right, Gus. She probably does charity work on weekends and reads to the blind." She moved aside for Mercury and his charge, who had just come up the porch steps. "Hello, Mercury. I take it the boat was already out to sea?"

Mercury helped Rance Carlisle through the door and to a couch, where Rance collapsed, huffing and mumbling, "I'm fine, just fine."

To Maggie, Mercury answered, "By the time I got there, yes."

"It's this sea air, Marchand!" Rance puffed. "I tell you, no normal man could run down there without collapsing."

"Uh-huh," said Mercury noncommittally, although Maggie detected a trace of disgust in his voice. "I found Mr. Carlisle collapsed on the road. Took me a few minutes to bring him 'round. And by the time I sprinted down to the docks, the boat was gone."

"It wasn't my fault," said Rance, breathing a little easier, and motioning to Mrs. Friar for a glass of water. "I have a heart condition."

"Does this mean Mr. Weintrout won't be coming at *all*?" said Mr. Andrews.

Skirting the pile of luggage, Maggie crossed the lobby and said, "I don't believe so, Mr. Andrews. Might I see your invitation?"

Andrews eyed her curiously, but dug in his pocket and produced the envelope.

"Mr. Carlisle? Mercury? No, that's all right, Gus," she said, when the cowboy started to hunt for his, too. "I've already seen yours."

She spread the three invitations out. Except for the names, they were identical. She looked up at Mercury. "You were invited to receive an award from"—she looked down at the invitation again—"the Pinnacle Footracer Society?"

Smiling, he scratched the back of his neck. "Guess I'm not so important as I thought, am I?"

She handed the invitations back. "I'm willing to bet Phoebe's and the Kelloggs' are the same. Where are the Kelloggs, anyway?"

"Upstairs," said Mr. Andrews. "Which is where I'm going. I must say, I'm very disappointed. I had counted on bagging an elk."

From the background, Mrs. Friar piped up, "Not on this island. There haven't been any elk here for ten years. A few deer, yes. But no elk. Not anymore."

Andrews sputtered, "Well . . . well, what was Weintrout *thinking*, then?" and dramatically stormed up the stairs in a tweedy blur.

"Sure in a big toot to butcher somethin', ain't he?" Gus drawled, staring after him.

"Well, it seems to me that we have to get ourselves

organized,'' said Carlisle, from the couch. He tipped a pill into his hand, then swallowed it with a swig of water. ''Got to get up teams to do the cooking and the maid duties—that'd be the women, of course.''

He stuck the pill vial back into his coat pocket and sat up a little straighter. ''Miss Maguire, you can start organizing the towels and washcloths. I'll need three sets. And get started on dinner. Now, we'll need somebody to bring in the meat. Mrs. Friar said there were a few deer. I suppose we should vote, but I really think I ought to be in charge. Plenty of experience. Circle C—''

''Beef,'' said Grady, finishing off the apple. ''Please don't start, Carlisle.'' He tossed the core into a wastepaper basket.

Maggie was about to tell Mr. Rance Carlisle to bend over and she'd give him his towels, all right, but reason prevailed. ''Mrs. Friar?'' she said, ''what do you suggest?''

''Well, I suppose I could do some cooking,'' Mrs. Friar said, slowly. ''I used to be a cook way back, before I was promoted to housekeeper. Meals'll be at eight, one, and seven, and you'll eat what I give you. No orders, no menus. But I can't do all of it. You folks're gonna have to clean up after yourselves. I mean your rooms. Nobody goes in my kitchen who ain't on the payroll.''

Maggie nodded with relief and said, ''Fine with me.'' From the corner of her eye, she saw Grady make the sign of the cross and thankfully raise his eyes heavenward. He didn't need to be so damned happy about it. She couldn't help it if she'd never learned to cook.

''And nobody shoots any of my deer,'' Mrs. Friar went on. ''I've got 'em all named. This island ain't a hunting preserve, in spite of what that little pip-squeak, Andrews, thinks. And one more thing. I was born ugly. I can't help that part. And I had me a little apoplexy about three years ago that didn't make me any prettier. But me and my husband, Joe, ran this lodge for Mr. R.C. Tippet till Joe up and died six months and seven days ago, and I run it now.

Anybody doesn't like the way I look?'' She crossed her arms. ''Well, I do the cooking. They might get a little surprise.''

Grady snickered.

''I suppose you can entertain yourselves during the days,'' Mrs. Friar continued. ''There's lots of things to keep you busy. It's a vacation resort, after all. But I'd appreciate it if none of you went swimmin' alone, since there ain't no lifeguards. And check your firearms at the desk. I lost a guest once to a game of backgammon, and I don't intend it should happen again. Any questions?''

Grady and Maggie each shook their head. Carlisle started to protest, but Mercury stared at him until he mumbled, ''Fine. Just fine.''

Gus, on the steps, said, ''Sounds dandy, ma'am. If we're not gonna be eatin' till seven, I don't reckon anybody'd mind if I took me a little catnap?''

Nobody minded, and he went upstairs.

Maggie said, ''Grady, I think you and I should do the same.'' He started to protest, but she said, ''I really think you should rest, Grady, what with your wound and all.''

''My what?'' he said, then gripped his arm. ''Oh. My *wound*!'' He started toward the stairs, Maggie following.

They were on the second floor and halfway to their rooms, when she whispered, ''You're holding the wrong arm.''

He switched and grumbled, ''What are we doing, anyway? I was hoping to get Mercury interested in a game of chess. Fascinating man! Did you know that he once ran all the way from Denver to—''

''Hush,'' she said. They came to her door, and went inside. ''Grady,'' she said with a sigh, ''will you please stop thinking about Mercury? We weren't invited here by accident.''

He flopped on the bed. ''Indeed not,'' he said, scrunching a pillow under his arm. ''We were invited here by Lolo

Carré. Or Thomas Alva Edison. Whichever story you like best."

Maggie rolled her eyes and made a conscious effort not to slap him. She said, "We were invited by person or persons unknown. Just like everybody else. And it had to be the same person."

"Or persons," Grady said, staring at the ceiling.

"So," she said, trying to ignore him, "who invited us all to this island? He or she—"

"Or they," he broke in.

"Grady," she said, through clenched teeth, "let's just leave it 'he' for now, all right? Otherwise, I shall be called upon to toss you out the window."

Grady closed his eyes and smiled. "Yes, dear."

Maggie mumbled something not very nice under her breath, then went on. "All the invitations were sent by the same person. This same person had the money to send everyone tickets and reserve their rooms—if, indeed, he paid for them—"

"You don't know that yet," Grady said, from behind closed eyes. "And I'm not paying. They can shoot me, but I'm not paying."

"If anybody shoots you, Grady, it'll be me."

He smiled. "That's comforting."

"I'll clear it up at dinner," she continued. "Anyway, this same person arranged for everyone to come when the lodge was closed and there was no staff, when the boats would be gone, and when we couldn't get off the island."

Grady nodded. "I'll give you that."

"So this person must have a reason for picking the people he did. I mean, it couldn't have been at random. So the next question is: What do all of us have in common? What does Phoebe have in common with Rance, that they both have in common with Mercury. And us. And the Kelloggs and Gus and Mr. Andrews, and maybe Mrs. Friar, too."

Grady sat up. "I must say, Maggie, if you went to all

this trouble just to take my mind off Miriam, you've succeeded. Can we go home now?''

She looked at him and said one word: ''Boat.''

He lay back down. ''Maybe tomorrow.''

Maggie went to the window. Mercury Marchand was out on the lawn, flopped casually in a lawn chair, one arm dangling and stroking the white cat she'd seen when they had first emerged from the wood. Now what could she possibly have in common with a fiftyish footracer from the Territories? Or, for that matter, an oversexed, ill-mannered widow from Sacramento, or a pair of reclusive penny-dreadful writers?

Seven

THEY MET ROMAN AND TEMPERANCE KELLOGG AT dinner. Roman Kellogg, in his late forties, was a big, beefy, ruddy-complected man. He was quite easily the tallest person in the room, and nearly as big around as Carlisle. Dark, curly hair not only covered his head, but grew in profusion from his cheeks to form a monstrously bushy and untamed beard which trailed down his chest. He looked nothing at all like Maggie's idea of a writer—he looked, in fact, like he could barely spell—but his wife seemed hardly more equipped than he.

Temperance Kellogg, while not a tiny woman, seemed dwarfed by his bulk. She spoke nary a word to anyone, and kept her eyes down. Blond, slight, and fair-skinned, she would have been very pretty if not for a vaguely gray, sickly look. This was possibly brought on by her husband, Maggie thought as she greeted them, and introductions were made. Roman Kellogg had the look of a bully about him.

Considering the short notice, Mrs. Friar (who had retired to the kitchen once the table was suitably sagging), had done quite well. Lamps were lit in the first of the lodge's two dining halls, and one of the long tables therein was laid out with fine china and silver. Lining the table were platters heaped with carved ham and the remains of a cold chuck roast. Baked squash and boiled peas, roasted potatoes and sauteed mushrooms, with salt cellars and bread baskets and fruit compotes poked in the empty spaces filled out the table.

Conversation was confined to complaint, the diners being too intent on the odd circumstances of their lodging to do much else besides grumble. And, of course, eat. Gus asked for the grape scissors, Carlisle asked if there was any horseradish for the tenderloin and then grumbled about the servicc, and Phoebe Perch threw a fit about a spot on her spoon.

About halfway through, Maggie asked the Kelloggs if she might see their invitation.

''You, too, Miss Perch,'' she added. ''If you wouldn't mind.''

''I certainly do mind,'' said Pheobe, looking up from the mushrooms she was helping herself to. ''And anyway,'' she continued, dark eyes flashing angrily in the lamplight, ''I don't have it with me. That is, I threw it away. On the mainland.''

Liar, thought Maggie. When they'd first arrived at the lodge, she'd seen the thick buff edge of the invitation sticking up from the corner of Phoebe's handbag. Likely she didn't want to show it because she wanted no one to know who had invited her. Maybe he was socially prominent, or involved in politics. But Maggie said, ''A shame,'' and accepted the Kelloggs' printed invitation.

''What's this about?'' asked Roman Kellogg. ''Don't you want to see anyone else's?''

Maggie handed it back, satisfied it was the same as the others. Their's had come from the Greater Western Authors Association. They were to have given a lecture.

Maggie said, ''I've already had a look at everyone elses'. And as to what it's about, well, it is my opinion that all of this—the invitations, the boat being gone, the staff's absence—is no accident.''

''Amazing deduction,'' Grady whispered, sarcastically, behind his napkin. ''I'm boggled.''

Maggie chose to ignore him. "Did all of you receive tickets and paid reservations?"

Everyone nodded.

"From someone, or some organization," she added, thinking of the Kelloggs and Mercury, "that you couldn't say no to?"

Again there were nods and murmurs of agreement.

Carlisle said, "Do you mean to tell me that somebody tricked us up here? What the hell for?"

"Oh, hogwash!" said Roman Kellogg.

Maggie paid him no mind. "Yes, Mr. Carlisle. I believe it was the same 'somebody' in all cases."

"Ma'am?" Gus spoke up, from the end of the table. " 'Scuse me for sayin' so, but that's plain silly. I ain't never met none of these folks afore in my life."

"That's right," said Phoebe, putting her napkin on her plate. "Why don't you stop all this foolishness, anyway. Let a man take charge."

Grady stood up. "I think," he said softly, "this is as good a time as any to leave."

"Coward," hissed Maggie. Then, in a louder voice, she said, "No one has taken charge, as Miss Perch puts it. However, I think—"

"Miss Maguire," said Roman Kellogg, "you'll pardon me for saying it, but nobody gives a fig what you think. I just want to find a boat and get off this rock. I could have had three chapters written in the time I've spent traveling, and—"

"Shut up, Kellogg," cut in Mr. Andrews. "Miss Maguire has at least been trying to reason out our plight. All Mr. Carlisle has been doing—and you look to be cut from the same cloth—is to make a great deal of noise. And no one here has the slightest interest in those horse operas you write."

"I do," said Gus, shyly, from his end of the table. "Why, I've read about all of 'em!" He blushed. "Honest, I think they're real good, Mr. Kellogg. I 'specially liked the one where Mesa Mike is trapped by them Kiowa, and he sends up that smoke signal that gets the cavalry a-comin', and then the—''

Abruptly, Phoebe Perch stood up. ''You are all ridiculous! I've never met such ridiculous people in my life! I'm going to my room.''

Maggie said, ''Miss Perch!''

The young woman wheeled. ''What!''

''I was just going to tell you to lock your—''

''Maggie?'' It was Grady, poking his head in from the next room, his expression bright and somewhat agitated and extremely eager. He looked, in fact, the way he had the first time he and Otto had got the plumbing to work right. ''Maggie,'' he said, ''I think you ought to hear this. You should all hear it.''

''Hear what?'' said Phoebe, plainly irritated.

Grady said, ''If everyone will come this way, please? I really insist.''

When Maggie reached the doorway, she pulled him aside. ''What's going on?'' she whispered.

''I found an Edison,'' he whispered back, smugly.

''And you brought everyone in here to hear a scratchy recording of someone reciting 'Mary Had a Little Lamb?' '' she asked, dryly. She had supposed, at the very least, that he'd found a body.

Smiling, he put his arm around her shoulder and practically towed her into the room. It was a smallish gaming suite, fitted with sofas and chairs, and tables for cards and backgammon and mah-jongg, and banked with windows on two sides. There was a bar against one wall, and Carlisle was already helping himself. He took his whiskey and sat down, and Mr. Andrews replaced him at the bar. ''Anyone else?'' Grady asked, staring pointedly at Carlisle.

Carlisle wasn't paying attention, though. He said, ''I'm listening. Hurry up about it.''

Grady turned up another lamp, and another, until the

room was quite bright. Maggie perched on the arm of an upholstered chair and waited with the others, trying all the while to decide whether to kill Grady now or wait until they went upstairs.

"While the rest of you were finishing your dinner argument," he began, "I wandered into this room—rather nice, don't you think?"

"Get on with it, Maguire," grumbled Kellogg, accepting a drink from Andrews. Maggie didn't see Mrs. Kellogg at first, then spied her in the corner, biting her lip. Pheobe was closer, standing by herself, arms crossed, a surly expression on her face. The slight motion of her skirts told Maggie that she was tapping her toe impatiently.

"Certainly, Kellogg," Grady replied brightly. "While I was in here, I stumbled across this." He stepped away to reveal an Edison, shiny and faintly alien. "It's one of Mr. Edison's talking machines."

"Say!" said Mercury, leaning forward. "That's quite a contraption! Does it work?"

"It certainly does," Grady said, and Maggie thought he looked as proud as if he, himself, had invented it. "However, I think you're all going to be surprised at the recording. You see, there was only one cylinder. I played it, of course. I'll play it again, but I warn you, you'll have to be very quiet. It's rather faint and scratchy."

"Oh, just shut up and crank the blasted thing, Maguire!" grumbled Carlisle.

Grady looked at Maggie and rolled his eyes, and then he began to turn the crank.

There was a second or two of static, and then a man's voice, made tinny and thin by the instrument, announced, "Sorry about the boat, but you see, I couldn't allow you to leave the island. And really, it was much nicer than blowing it up, which is what would have happened had you caught the captain in time.

"I wonder, should I tell you who I am? It might be more

amusing if you didn't know. But no, I'll take pity on you. By Wednesday, when the boat comes again, you'll all have been killed by your old friend Sam Warden. I'm right here, among you. I'll be seeing you all, one last time.''

EIGHT

AFTER A FEW SECONDS THAT WERE EMPTY, SAVE FOR the scratching of the needle, Grady stopped cranking, and Maggie tore her gaze away from the Edison to look at the other guests.

Temperance Kellogg had fainted, and Roman was busily patting her cheek. Pheobe had collapsed into a chair, looking stricken. Carlisle just sat there, not noticing he'd dropped his glass on the rug.

"What's the meaning of this, Maguire?" asked Andrews, stepping forward. Maggie thought he looked a little pale.

Grady shrugged, and Maggie said, "I believe his meaning was quite clear, Mr. Andrews. He's here to kill us, and he's one of us."

"He's gonna kill us?" Gus piped up, and for the first time, his expression was less than affable. "What the heck for? Well, I don't know about the rest of y'all, but I never heard of no Mr. Sam Warden. I was invited here by my old buddy, Smiley Dowd, to set up a bona fide business deal, and I intend to by God find out what happened to him. I'm gettin' my Colt back from that lady at the desk, too!"

As Gus left the room, boots thumping across the carpet, Phoebe stood up again. One hand on the back of her chair—Maggie would have sworn it was the only thing holding her up—Phoebe said, "Ludicrous," but her voice wavered. "Someone's playing a nasty joke on us, that's all. I am simply astonished at the lengths . . . the lengths . . . to which . . ." Her eyes closed, and she crumpled to the floor, as if she were a marionette and someone had simply cut her strings.

Andrews immediately went to her side, then looked up, accusingly, at Grady. "See what you've done, Maguire? I don't know why you played that filthy machine in the first place. You could have had the decency to have wait until the ladies retired. Sir, you are no gentleman!" He patted Phoebe's hand. "Miss Perch? Miss Perch, can you hear me?"

When she didn't answer, he scooped her up into his arms, staggering slightly, even though she was a tiny woman, and carried her from the room, calling, "Mrs. Friar! Mrs. Friar, come help me!"

The Kelloggs followed directly, Roman helping his wife, who stumbled along under his supporting arm. "I have to agree with Andrews, Maguire. Bad show all around. You ought to be horsewhipped."

Grady opened his mouth, then seemed to think better of it and closed it again with a click.

Maggie said, "My goodness." Only Mercury and Carlisle remained, Carlisle in an apparent state of shock. Mercury just looked thoughtful. To Grady, she said, "Well, you certainly know how to clear a room."

He sat down. "Thanks. I guess. I find it interesting that nobody admits to knowing Sam Warden, though, don't you?"

Actually, she found it more interesting that he was taking a genuine interest in the case. She would have preferred getting him over Miriam Cosgrove by some simpler means—fishing or gin rummy or a pretty young lady. But she supposed you worked with what you had at hand. She said, "Mr. Carlisle? Every heard of Sam Warden?"

Carlisle looked up from the bottle of pills with which he

was fumbling. He jammed one into his mouth, and then, so softly that she had to lean forward to hear him, he said, ''I don't feel so good. I wonder, that is, could somebody . . .''

Maggie glanced at Mercury, then Grady, and made her choice. ''Grady, would you please help Mr. Carlisle upstairs?'' Grady gave her an odd look, but helped the man to his feet.

Maggie watched them leave. They had just gone through the door and turned out of sight, when Mercury said, ''You're a real take-charge gal, aren't you, Miss Maguire?''

She turned to face him, and saw that he was smiling. ''I suppose I am. I don't know how to be any other way.''

He moved closer and settled on the sofa. ''No need to apologize, not that I think you were, mind. My wife's the same. She thinks something needs doing or fixing, and she's the first to say so. And the first to delegate the doing or fixing, too.'' His smile widened. ''You going to ask me whether I've ever heard of Sam Warden?''

Maggie said, ''Well, yes, if you don't mind. Everybody else left before I had a chance.''

Mercury leaned back on the sofa, spreading his long arms out along its back, his immaculately tailored dinner jacket gaping slightly. ''I've heard of him, all right. It's been a long time, but a feller doesn't forget a thing like that.''

Maggie slid the rest of the way into the chair. ''Do go on.''

Mercury stuck his legs out before him and lolled his head back, looking either like the portrait of contentment or the picture of crucifixion, Maggie thought—an odd juxtaposition. ''It was nearly twenty-five years back,'' he began, ''and I was just a kid. Well, not a kid really. Just seems that way now.''

He pursed his lips. ''I guess I was about twenty-seven or so, and I was living in Maplethorpe, Kansas. I'd just married my Eliza. I had a tailoring business, too, but it wasn't doing too good. Not much need for gentlemen's suits in a farming town. Not many fancy dinners.'' He fingered his lapel for a moment, then leaned over and reached for a water pitcher. ''You mind? Ham was awful salty.''

''Not at all,'' said Maggie. She had to hand it to his Eliza. He certainly was well-trained. Casual, yet polite. Gracious. And then she had to take it back. Men like Mercury were born, not groomed. She liked him.

He poured his glass of water, took a swallow, then settled back again. ''Anyway, there were some fellers over to Holt—the town's gone now, but it was good-sized then—that had heard about my running. They came to me and asked would I be interested in a footrace, but not just any footrace—a real long distance marathon race. East, from Kickapoo Springs—that's gone, now, too—to Topeka. It was a distance of over forty miles.''

''Heavens!'' said Maggie, under her breath.

He heard, and smiled. ''I said something a little more forceful, I think. Anyway, they had my competition all picked out for me. Lightning Louie Pasternak, from up around St. Paul. I don't know if you ever heard of him, but—''

''I have,'' said Grady, leaning in the doorway. They both turned to look at him. ''Fastest man in the Northwest. Well, what was Northwest back then. May I?'' He entered the room and settled in a chair opposite Mercury.

Maggie said, ''You get Rance put to bed?''

Grady nodded. To Mercury, he said, ''Please, don't let me stop you. Go on.''

''Well, they were offering a lot of money,'' Mercury went on. ''I think the purse was a hundred and fifty dollars, which was enough to get me and Eliza moved and started up somewhere else, fresh. It was mighty appealing. And I was pretty sure I could beat this Lightning Louie. I'd never raced against him, but I'd heard he was a little feller, one of those stringy sprinter types.'' He looked at Maggie. ''That's a short distance man. Anyway, I said yes.''

He took a sip of water, then grinned wide. ''The man

who came to me, who made the offer to run? That was Sam Warden. He owned the Prairie Belle Saloon in Holt. Well, it was more like a gamblin' palace. Roulette, poker, faro. And ladies, of course. An oasis in the desert, he called it, though I guess he'd never been out west—really out west—to see the real thing."

A chuckle escaped Maggie. "I suppose not. Did you win the race?"

"Now, see, you're just like Eliza," he said, grinning. "Always wantin' to jump ahead in the story. 'For God's sake, get to the point, Morris!' she's always saying. I reckon I do go on . . ." He shook his head.

"Well, anyway, to make a long story short, I just about didn't finish it. About eight miles out of Kickapoo Springs, where we started, somebody commenced to shooting at me. I was just sort of lopin' when it happened, still had plenty of reserve left on account of I had let that idiot, Lightning Louie, tear on ahead of me. I figured to let him tire himself out early. But when those shots started comin', I lit out like the devil himself was on my tail. Went off the road and up into these rocks to hide, and pretty soon here came these two yahoos, doggin' my trail with their rifles pulled out. I knew somethin' was up."

Grady leaned forward. "You were the favorite. Of course! Warden bet against you, didn't he?"

Mercury nodded. "Warden and all of his cronies. Figured that out later on, but right then I was just plain mad."

Maggie found that she was sitting on the edge of her chair. "What happened next?"

"I was young and stupid," Mercury went on. "I didn't think twice. I jumped down on top of those two fellers—they were right under me—and I'll be damned if I didn't fall just right and bang their heads together."

He slapped his hands together, and Maggie jumped. "They were out cold—dumb luck, of course—but I recognized one of 'em as a young gamecock that worked for Warden. So I took up their horses' reins and just kept running. Figured they'd have a good long walk in to town.''

Grady raised his brow. ''You didn't climb up on a horse and head for safety?''

Mercury appeared shocked. ''I was runnin' a race! That would have been cheating. Besides, I was of a mind to show Sam Warden and his cronies what an honest racer could do. See, I'd figured it out by then. And I guess I was stupid. You get this sort of, well, euphoria when you're runnin'. It's hard to explain. But you figure you can beat the world.

''I guess maybe another two miles or so down the pike I came to a water station they'd set up. I left the horses with the folks there and told 'em what had happened, in case somebody else took another shot at me and didn't miss.

''Nothin' else happened until about seven, maybe six miles outside'a Topeka, when I came across Lightning Louie, just keeled over. Poor little feller. Wasn't used to the Kansas summers, I expect. Anyway, I carried him a couple miles before I found some people with a wagon, and then I ran on in by myself. I reckon that on that day, Sam Warden lost not only the Prairie Belle, but most everything he owned. I got my purse, though, and me and Eliza lit out, but he was looking for me for a good long spell. Had to move three times.''

Mercury toyed with a seam in his pant leg, then looked up at Maggie. ''Guess he found me, didn't he?''

NINE

AFTER MERCURY WENT UPSTAIRS, MAGGIE HAD Grady crank the cylinder for her again. He didn't mind, not the second time or the third. The machine was fascinating in its simplicity, and he mentally kicked himself because *he* hadn't thought of it.

"I could have been a millionaire," he grumbled, grinding the crank. His shoulder was beginning to hurt.

"Shh!" Maggie said, listening.

At last she'd had enough, and she helped him blow out the lamps. They went upstairs to her room.

"Close the door," she said, lighting a lamp.

"Dear heavens," Grady said, already latching the door behind him. He flopped in a chair. "What will people think?"

"Frankly," said Maggie, perching on the bed, "I don't much care what this bunch thinks."

He took off his glasses and began to polish them. "Except for Mercury. May I remind you, my dear, that he's married?"

"Grady!"

He chuckled. She'd turned bright pink. He'd hit a nerve. "His wife will probably hire your counterpart to surprise you, in flagrante delicto." And then he thought about her suitor from Western Mutual Specialties Insurance, and said, "What will Quincy Applegate make of it, I wonder? Ah, what a lovely mess. There'll be press, of course.'' His hands, spectacles dangling, drew out a banner in the air. '' 'Distaff Dick Nabbed with Racing Romeo.' Quite the headline!''

He gave a last swipe to his glasses, then settled them back on his nose. Smiling smugly, he stared at her.

When she didn't reply, he said, ''What?''

''I was just wondering,'' she said, the flush fading from her cheeks, ''how a pickpocket from the Barbary Coast ever came to learn Latin. Did you snatch it up out of somebody's purse?''

''Nope,'' he said, swinging his feet up on the ottoman. ''Learned it in court.''

''Well, for your information, I think Mercury Marchand is a very nice man. And that's all. He's one of the only nice people on this island. Gus is all right, too. And I don't suppose it's fair to have an opinion about Temperance Kellogg yet, seeing as how she hasn't spoken a word. But these others?'' She made a face. ''You'll notice I didn't include you with the nice people. And leave Quincy out of this.''

''Yes, Mags,'' he said, smiling. It was a cliché, but she *was* pretty when she was angry.

''Can you be serious for five minutes, Grady?''

He crossed his arms and put on his best Chester A. Arthur face. ''Starting now,'' he said.

''That Edison. Does a person need any extra equipment to make it record? I mean, can you do it on the machine without a lot of bother?''

What was she getting at? He said, ''Basically, you just put in a fresh cylinder and speak into the trumpet. And turn the crank, of course.''

''Could one man do it alone?''

He shrugged. ''It would be easier with two, but yes, a person could do it by himself. Where are you going with this?''

She stared not at him, but at a picture on the wall.

He said, ''I don't understand what all the fuss is about.

Obviously, it's just somebody playing a trick. Sam Warden can't kill anybody. He's dead."

Maggie shook her head. "Don't be so sure. They never did find his body, did they?"

"That's true. But San Quentin . . ."

"They never found his body, Grady. And that recording had to have been made within ninety minutes—between the time the boat sailed without us, and when we all came down for dinner. The cylinder was very specific. It said, 'Sorry about the boat, but it was better than blowing it up,' or something like that. I think it was Sam Warden, and I think he was telling us the truth. He's here."

Grady leaned forward. "All right. I can understand how we'd walk right past him and not know him. I mean, everything that went into catching him was long distance. Paperwork. Sending telegrams."

Maggie smiled a little. "One of our more convenient cases . . ."

"But what about everybody else?" Grady went on. "Wouldn't one of them have recognized him if he was standing right in front of them?"

Maggie shrugged. "Not necessarily. Warden was known for his disguises. Well, after a certain point in his career, anyway. We don't know how much time has passed since he's seen them. In Mercury's case, it's been almost twenty-five years. So tell me, Grady. Tell me everything we know about Sam Warden."

Grady grimaced. Every time she made him do this, he felt like a trained poodle in her father's circus. He closed his eyes and concentrated, and then he began to speak.

"Sam Warden. Alias Sam Jeffreys, Jefferson Samuels, Joe Warburger, Joseph Warden, and others too numerous to mention. Born in Cincinnati, 1833; some sources say '31, others say Brooklyn, 1827. Started out as a petty thief, moved up to house sneak and burglar. In and out of jail repeatedly. Broke out of Dannemora Prison, New York, in 1853, and disappeared. Not heard of until—well, Mercury's encounter is a year earlier than I had before."

Maggie leaned her weight on one arm. "Get to the more recent stuff, Grady. Actually, just a description, for now."

No *How on earth do you remember that, Grady?* or *Thank you for sharing your amazing mental prowess.* Or better yet, *Grady, you're a god!* No, just *Get to the more recent stuff.*

It was hell, being underappreciated.

With a sigh, he began again. "Reports conflict. Sam Warden is described as being anywhere from five-foot-eight to five-foot-eleven, and having blond, sandy, light brown or dark brown hair. Two witnesses described it as red. Undoubtedly, he dyed it frequently. He has blue, green, brown or hazel eyes. Even the prison records disagree. Personally, I vote for hazel. Warden's alternately clean-shaven or wears a full beard, and everything in between. Within a certain broad range, he seems to be a chameleon."

"Which is why we caught him by tracing records on that phony bank stock deal," Maggie said.

"Precisely. In recent years, Warden was wanted for wagon theft and till-tapping—must have had a few off years. But mostly for confidence work, ranging from neat and tidy to despicable. He seems to have run the gamut during his career. People who crossed him tended to disappear, if you get my drift."

Maggie nodded. "And you have to wonder just how much he got away with. The crimes that aren't on the books, I mean, because the victims were too embarrassed. Or too dead."

Grady stifled a yawn. He was looking forward to climbing into his own bed and cozying up with the copy of *The New Inventor* he'd brought along. "I still say it's a fake. Somebody having their little joke. Warden's dead as a stump, and he's not coming back."

"No," said Maggie. "It's too elaborate. I think he's going to make good on his word. You're acting as if you're a bystander in this, Grady. I remind you that you helped put him in San Quentin five years ago. Fifteen years was the best the jury could do. Of course, he only served two years of it.''

Grady scowled theatrically. ''The piker. Let's hang him.''

''Don't be so smug,'' Maggie said. ''You're on his list, too.''

He waved a finger at her. ''I remind you, the invitation was in your name.''

''It came,'' she said, standing up, ''with tickets for two. Now I ask you—who else would I have brought along?''

He stood, too. ''Otto?''

She opened the door.

''Quincy? Oh, all right, I'm going.''

''Yes, do,'' she said, fairly shoving him out into the hall. ''And take your dirty mind with you. Quincy, indeed.''

He crossed the hall and unlocked his door, and as he stepped inside, she said, ''Grady?''

''Yes.''

''I'd lock that behind me, if I were you.''

He smiled at her. ''Yes, Mags.''

He waited to go in until she'd shut her door and he heard the key turn, and then he waited a bit longer, listening. Actually, he agreed with Maggie. Everything was just too finely tuned, too macabre—and too bloody expensive—to be somebody's idea of a joke. Sam Warden hadn't drowned in the San Francisco Bay. His body hadn't been swept out to sea or eaten by sharks. Those had been the popular theories. No, he had crawled up out of that bay three years ago, and he'd been keeping his head low and plotting his revenge ever since.

He stared down at the key in his hand. He could put thirty more locks on his door, but if Sam Warden—lock-pick, sneak thief, confidence man, and murderer—wanted him, it still wouldn't be enough.

Finally, he heard what he'd been listening for: the soft, rhythmic *smacks* of rubber balls hitting palms. Maggie was juggling. Maggie was thinking. Perhaps all was not right with the world, but Maggie was trying to fix it. He allowed himself a little smirk. It really must be galling her that nobody was paying her for this.

He was just about to go inside when he heard something else, something drifting around the corner of the hall. Quietly, he crept toward the sound, through the darkness, until he found himself outside the Kelloggs' door.

Weeping, that's what it was, the sound of weeping. Temperance Kellogg. And over it, he heard Roman Kellogg say, "Shut up, will you? I can't stand it anymore! Just finish the goddamn chapter and come to bed. We're behind. We're not going to meet our deadline!"

"But he's come to kill us!" Temperance Kellogg said. At least, Grady assumed it was Temperance. He hadn't heard her speak before.

"Bullshit," said Roman. "Why would he kill us over a damn character in a book? I'm going to keep on using Salty Bob, and that's all there is to it. Now, start writing."

"But Roman—"

"I said, shut up and write!"

Grady waited a moment, but there was nothing more forthcoming, other than an occasional sniffle from Temperance, and he slowly felt his way back to his room. He wished now that he'd read the Kelloggs' books. Actually, he had read a couple, but none that included any Salty Bob, and he'd stopped reading them because they were so flowery. Never used one adjective where six would do, never a verb without an adverb or three.

It wore on the reader after a time.

Well, Gus said he'd read them. He'd have a little chat with him in the morning. And Maggie, too.

TEN

AT 11:00 P.M., PHOEBE PERCH AWOKE IN HER ROOM, wondering how she'd got there. Then she remembered with a shudder. That sonofabitch Sam was really here, and she'd be damned if she could tell which one he was. Too many years. Six? Seven? Too many disguises.

He could change his voice, appear taller or shorter. No one could detect the putty noses he crafted, the chins, the brow ridges. He lodged cotton in his cheeks on occasion, sometimes even wires, and could make his ears appear bigger or smaller or stick out like an elephant's. He could even change the color of his eyes.

She should know. She'd seen him transform.

Muttering, "Crikey," she got up, jammed a chair under the doorknob, then viciously tore her invitation into tiny pieces and threw it in the wastebasket. And then, with trembling fingers, she started to unpin her hair.

By that same time, A. M. Andrews was sound asleep and dreaming about *Hamlet*, of all things. In the dream, he entered, stage right, and suddenly realized he'd forgotten his speech.

He woke in a cold sweat, crossed the room in the dark, and poured himself a glass of water and added a sleeping powder, wondering just what in heaven's name he'd gotten himself into. ''You've bitten off more than you can chew this time, old man,'' he whispered to himself, then downed the glass.

After a few minutes of sitting on the edge of his bed, turning the guest list over and over in his head, he returned to his bed and sank into a deep sleep which, this time, was untroubled by dreams.

In the dark of his room, Gus Thorpe sat on the edge of his bed, eyes focused on the long, thin, vertical stripe of pale moonlight let in by the curtains.

If Maggie or any of the other guests could have seen him at that moment, they would have been surprised, to say the least. For neither Augustus Thorpe's face nor demeanor suggested anything of the cowboy he purported to be. His eyes were hard and cold and crafty, his motions calculated, and his shoulders were hunched into a tense knot as he sat, stubbing out his ready-made cigarette in a tray that already sported seven squashed butts.

''Shit,'' he muttered under his breath, for the third time in the last hour. ''What a goddamned pisser.''

Then he angrily reached for the pack, and lit himself another smoke.

In the Kelloggs' room, Roman was asleep and snoring loudly. Temperance was at the desk. Her pen lay before her, her sentence half-finished, and her head was in her hands.

She was weeping. Weeping because she'd never finish the chapter before midnight, not one that Roman would like, anyway. Weeping because Roman snored. Weeping because she had this sense of impending doom. And most of all, weeping because Sam Warden had come back, come back after her with a sword in his hand and revenge on his mind, after so many years.

It was one thing for him to write those letters to Roman, making demands, asking for money. He'd never so much as mentioned her name. She thought she was safely anonymous.

But he was here. He was here, and he was after her. She'd thought, after all, that she should be able to see through his disguise.

She'd been wrong.

She cried softly for a little while longer, and then picked up the pen again. She waited until her hand stopped shaking. Mustn't tremble. Roman would know something was wrong and beat her for it.

After a bit, she slipped into the bathroom and took a fresh bottle from the neat row of their things. She broke the seal, opened it, and drank. Just a sip. Maybe three. Three would settle her. Four, and she'd pass out. Mustn't swoon.

The moment the laudanum passed her lips, she began to relax. Recapping it, she settled it precisely in the row from which she'd removed it, and repaired once again to the bedroom.

Back at the desk, she again dipped her pen in the inkwell, and slowly, carefully, returned to the adventures of the dashing Mesa Mike, and his nemesis, the evil Salty Bob Waters as Roman's snores slowly faded into the soft background of liquid opium.

It would come to her, what to do. Plots always came to her, she told herself as the drug took its full effect. She already knew what to do, but the question was when. And could she, really, when it came right down to it?

She thought so.

Down the hall, Rance Carlisle was suspended in that place between waking and sleep. A smile was on his lips, and a faint humming sound rose from them occasionally. He was half-dreaming of a marching band, and he was humming the tune they played as they marched: "The Rose of Dundee." Actually, in the dream, he was singing full bore, at the top of his lungs, as he led the band, which was composed of instrument-playing cattle, all with a gigantic black Circle C brand.

Suddenly the street vanished, and the crowd, and there appeared before him a gigantic metal hooded contraption, wide as the cattle band, big as a barn, that went back into blackness and made a whirring sound.

As he led the band nearer, he stepped to the side, cheering the cattle on, knees pumping in time with the music, listening to the screams and cries as whirling blades connected with meat and sinew and bone. But the cattle never faltered. They calmly marched on, into the blades.

And then the cattle changed to people, the people at the lodge, and they, too, walked gaily into the jaws of the machine: Maggie Maguire playing a trumpet, Gus Thorpe wielding a xylophone and so on.

And then the bawling of cattle changed to the terrified shrieks of people. A jagged piece of Roman Kellogg's tuba came flying out, then Phoebe Perch's bloody hand, still clutching her piccolo.

And the music stopped.

A big bass drum appeared at Carlisle's side. He picked it up and, drumming for all he was worth, followed the rest into the gory abattoir.

He was grinning like an idiot.

Downstairs, Mrs. Friar had finished putting away the dishes and had gone to her room after an exhausting search for a piece of cutlery. Funny. She could have sworn it was on the table, but it was nowhere to be found. Not in the drawer. Nowhere.

She undressed, then braided her hair. That was still difficult, getting it braided straight, but her arm was behaving better all the time now. Right after the stroke she hadn't been able to move it more than a few inches.

Stepping over the cat, she went to the closet and brought out her late husband's rifle. Loading it, she laid it atop the bedclothes on his side of the bed, then went around and crawled in on hers with a "Kitty, kitty? Come to bed, Albatross."

These people were all crazy. And a woman alone couldn't be too careful.

The cat jumped up, and purring, settled himself in the valley between the pillows. Mrs. Friar blew out the lamp and settled back. One hand gently resting on the rifle's stock, she sank into sleep.

Mercury Marchand crept quietly down the stairs without benefit of a candle, groping his way along the bannister. Soundlessly, he entered the dining room, where the drapes were thrown open to the pewter moonlight. No light shone from under the kitchen door at the far end. Good.

He slipped into the game room, carefully closing the door behind him, and went to the Edison. Grady had left the cylinder in place. That was good, too.

He went to the corner and felt around for the medicine clubs he'd seen earlier. He lifted one, carried it back to the machine, and sat down.

Slowly, he began to turn the crank, and the thin, crackly tones began: "Sorry about the boat, but you see, I couldn't allow you to leave the island . . ."

ELEVEN

AT SEVEN A.M. ON THE DOT, MAGGIE AWOKE. SHE sat bolt upright in bed, eyes wide, and breathed, "Suds!"

She leapt out of bed and pulled on her wrapper, only noticing on her way to the door that it was inside out, then paused with her hand on the knob. No. Get dressed first, that was the ticket. Just hurry!

She raced though her toilet, threw on her clothes, and was pounding on Grady's door in fifteen minutes.

He answered it in his nightshirt. "What?" Then, "Maggie?"

She shoved her way past him and waited until he closed the door. "I've got it!" she almost shouted. "I know who he is!"

Grady was looking at her oddly. "Maggie, what in God's name have you done to your hair?"

From habit, she raised her hand and patted at it, then dropped it in disgust. "Grady, aren't you *listening* to me? I said, I know who Sam Warden is!"

He sat down in an armchair. "All right, I'll bite. Who?"

She crossed her arms and grinned. "Mr. Andrews."

He screwed up his face. "You've got to be joking."

"Grady, think about it! He told us his name was A. M. Andrews, right?"

"So?"

She threw up her hands in exasperation. "It's an anagram, you dolt! Sam Warden equals A. M. Andrews. Just scramble the letters!"

Grady stood up. "By God! It wasn't elk he was going to shoot, it was us." He started for the door.

Maggie raced ahead of him and blocked it. "Grady, might I remind you that you're in your nightshirt? Get dressed. Plus, I think I want to announce this at breakfast. Strength in numbers and all that."

Grady shook his head. "You just want to show up Rance Carlisle."

She smiled. "That, too."

"Well, fix your hair first. It's . . . funny."

She patted it again. He was right. It did feel a little lopsided. "All right," she said. "I'll meet you in the hall in . . . ?"

"In twenty minutes," he replied, and opened the door for her.

"Well, at least it's even now," Grady whispered twenty-five minutes later, as he pulled out her chair at the dining table.

"Shhh," Maggie said, and willed herself not to fuss at her hair. She'd quickly (and sloppily) pulled the drooping, pinned rats from it and settled for a knot at the back of her head.

The Kelloggs were there ahead of them, Temperance looking even more frail than last night. Grady mumbled, "Good morning." Maggie followed suit, then turned her attention to the doorway. While she tapped her index finger on the table in anticipation, the other guests wandered in. Phoebe looked as elegant and spoiled as she had the previous day. Mercury nodded happily and immediately asked for the toast rack to be passed. By the time the clock struck eight, that sanctimonious weasel, Rance Carlisle, had joined them. They were only short A. M. Andrews and Gus, who, by five past the hour, still hadn't joined them. Mrs. Friar began serving.

Maggie had a very uneasy feeling. Andrews was Warden, wasn't he? You'd have thought he'd be the first at the table, to secretly gloat over his future victims. And Gus. Where was Gus? Suddenly, Maggie was gripped with a feeling of impending doom. Could Andrews have killed Gus? Gus was a scrapper. He'd put up a fight. Maybe Andrews was killing him now—or trying to!

She stood up. "Grady, would you please come with me?"

To the sound of Grady's chair legs scraping, Maggie walked with apparent leisure toward the stairs, so as not to alarm the other guests. Andrews was killing Gus, and she could have prevented it if she hadn't been so bloody set on showing up Rance Carlisle at the breakfast table!

At the stairs she put on speed and raced upward. Grady followed, waving his napkin and shouting between breathless huffs, "What is it?" and "Slow down!"

Maggie skidded to a halt in front of Gus's door, pounding on it with her fist as she commanded, "Check Andrews."

When Gus didn't answer, she pulled a pin from her hair, knelt, and went to work on the lock. Down the hall, Grady (who hadn't had any luck, either) hissed, "What are you doing?"

She glanced up, then back at the lock. She almost had it. "What's it look like?"

"They probably just went for a walk and lost track of the time. You're breaking and entering!"

"Yes," she said, as the lock turned over and the door creaked open a hair. She smiled triumphantly. "Yes, I am."

To the sound of Grady grumbling and slapping his pockets for his lock-pick kit, she slowly pushed open the door, prepared for the worst.

There was nothing. No blood-soaked corpse. No dangling corpse. No one shot dead in the bathroom or bleeding into the tub. No feet sticking up from the water closet. Andrews had not struck.

She felt, well, vaguely embarrassed.

"Suds," she said softly, and turned. Right into Rance Carlisle.

"Just what the devil do you think you're doing, Miss Maguire?" he said, face red with indignation. Or maybe it was just the effort of climbing the stairs. "This room belongs to the cowboy, as I recall. That Gus feller. Back home, we respect a hand's privacy."

Maggie pushed past him, muttering, "I notice you're in here, too," and after he followed her out, closed the door behind them and started toward Andrews's room. The door was open, so Grady was inside.

"This is no business for a female," Carlisle continued, hot on her heels as she turned into Andrews's room. "Why don't you just go back down to the table and let a man—"

Carlisle shut his mouth, midsentence, when he ran into Maggie's back. She had halted abruptly, and Carlisle nearly bowled her over. She was too shaken to do much besides regain her balance and take in the scene before her.

Grady stood at the end of the bed. On it was Andrews, his sheets and nightshirt stained rusty brown with dried blood. He had been stabbed through the heart, apparently sometime during the night. Long enough ago for his blood to have dried. There was quite a bit of blood, still thick and damp at the site of the wound.

"Good Lord," Carlisle whispered. She heard him move backward and sink into a chair.

Grady looked up. "Somebody else figured out . . ." He caught sight of Carlisle. "Your, um, theory, Mags."

She moved to the bedside for a closer look. "It would seem so." There was only one hole in the nightshirt, the one that had admitted the blade. The killer had plunged the knife home on the first strike. Death had been instantaneous, for there was no sign that Andrews had fought back or even stirred.

The knife, which she did not touch, was an uncommon one. It was, in fact, a carving knife, one with the Wapiti Lodge logo on its grip. The one that had been on the ham platter at dinner last night, if she remembered correctly.

Without looking up from the body, she said, "The door wasn't locked, was it?"

Grady replied, "No. And after I went to all the trouble of finding my kit, too."

"What's going on in—Oh my!" Maggie whirled just in time to see Mrs. Friar, who had just entered, faint dead away.

Maggie stared at the floor for a moment before she said, "Do something about that, Grady. Oh, wait." She dug in her pocket and came up with a key. "Here. Put her in my room. Mr. Carlisle?"

He was still in the chair, white-faced and shaking, and she prayed he wouldn't have a coronary right there. She couldn't carry him, for one thing. She knelt beside him, and said, "Mr. Carlisle? Rance? Would you like me to help you to your room?"

Staring at the body, Carlisle whispered, "This wouldn't happen at the Circle C," more to himself than Maggie, really, and then he slowly stood up. Louder, in a voice that trembled slightly, he said, "No thanks, little lady. I'll see to myself. Just a little trouble with the old ticker."

Maggie ground her teeth at that "little lady" business, but let it pass. She was too distracted by the corpse on the bed, and wondering which of the lodge's other inhabitants had killed him. Nine possibilities. Seven, actually, not counting herself or Grady.

She went to the door and watched as Rance Carlisle falteringly made his way to his room. He might be a misogynist swine, but if she was any judge of character, he had been quite honestly shaken. Count him out, too. That made six suspects.

And Mrs. Friar? The weapon was a carving knife from her kitchen, although it could have been lifted from the table by anyone. Still, she could have faked that collapse. Perhaps she was an actress, hired by Warden to—No, that was silly. For starters, no one would ever pay her to appear in public with that face.

A corner of Maggie's mouth crooked up. Her father might have paid for that face. He would have called her "Hideous Hildegard" or "Terrible Tondelayo" or some such name; dressed her in a grass skirt with bangles and bones, and would have made her face even worse with makeup. He would have charged a dime to people who wanted to see a "typical and ferocious native of far Peru"—or Borneo, or Tasmania, or else some unknown island whose name he made up on the spur of the moment—"who charge into battle unarmed, for they can literally scare their opponents to death with a look."

"Enjoying our work a little overmuch, are we?" Grady was back.

"What? Oh, nothing. Was Mrs. Friar really out?"

"Far as I could tell. Limp as a ragdoll. Why?"

Maggie glanced over her shoulder at Andrews. "I suppose we can count her out. For now. That puts us down to five suspects."

Grady said, "I trust you're not counting me among them?"

"No motive," replied Maggie, staring at the body again.

"Thanks," said Grady, dryly.

"All of whom," Maggie continued, "are downstairs at the moment, with the exception of Gus. I suggest we go back downstairs and break the news. Question everybody. We can go over the room more thoroughly later on. And Grady?"

Halfway out the door, he turned. "What?"

"Don't mention that thing about the anagram. I want to see if anybody comes up with it on their own."

Grady poked a thumb at Andrews. ''And what about him?''

''He's not going anywhere.'' She grabbed his key off the top of his bureau, then paused to look, for a moment, at something else.

''What?'' said Grady.

''This packet.'' She picked it up, and a powdery residue dusted the bureau's marble top. Maggie ran her finger through it, then brought finger to mouth. ''Well, he wasn't expecting it. That falls into my theory. Only a man with nothing to worry about would've had the brass to take a sleeping powder last night.''

Then she turned. ''Shall we?'' As she walked past Grady, she flipped him the key. ''Best lock the place up. For what little good it'll do.''

TWELVE

"THERE HAS BEEN . . . AN UNFORTUNATE INCIDENT," Maggie announced to the guests as Grady took his seat. The Kelloggs and Mercury looked up right away: Roman Kellogg was vaguely curious, Temperance appeared mortified, and Mercury was attentive and concerned. Phoebe didn't look up at all. She just kept primly eating her sausage and eggs.

Staring at Phoebe, Maggie said, "Mr. Andrews has been murdered."

Roman Kellogg came halfway out of his chair. "What!"

"Sit down, Mr. Kellogg," Maggie said.

"Just now?" asked Mercury. There was a thin thread of alarm in his voice. It was controlled, but Maggie heard it.

Phoebe, showing no emotion at all, was still eating. Her knife sliced into a sausage.

"Miss Perch? Did you hear me? Someone has murdered Mr. Andrews."

Phoebe's knife and fork were laid to rest on her plate at the proper angles. She patted her lips with her napkin, then turned her head toward Maggie and said, "I heard you. Do you expect tears? What was he to me? I barely had the man's acquaintance, after all."

If there was anything that bothered Maggie Maguire more than a condescending man, it was a cold, class-hopping woman, especially when she was as nasty as

Phoebe. She ground her teeth for the few seconds it took to push her anger back, and then said, ''Perhaps you should be the first to be questioned. If you'd care to step into the game room?''

Phoebe slapped her napkin down on the table and stood up. ''Questioned? I certainly will not be questioned like some common criminal! I don't see what gives you the right to come in here and take over! Who are you, anyway, besides an unmarried woman who travels to lodges with her 'cousin'? Don't think we don't see through your sham. I, for one, am going to my room.''

She slammed her chair back and turned to leave, but ran smack into Grady, who said with a scowl, ''I won't ask you to take that back, Miss Perch. You're under a strain. But you will go to the game room. And you will cooperate. Do you understand?''

Maggie bit her lips to hold the chuckle back. Grady had a bit of the actor in him, and he could look very menacing when the situation called for it. She had a feeling, though, that there wasn't that much acting involved this time.

Walking behind Phoebe, with his hands on her shoulders, Grady escorted her to the game room door. With a ''Humph!'' she threw him a withering glance and strode inside.

''Thanks,'' Maggie whispered.

''My distinct pleasure,'' said Grady, still scowling.

Maggie whispered, ''If you think the others will stay put, go upstairs and have a look through her room. The invitation's what I'm after. It's the only one I haven't seen.''

Grady nodded, and closed the door behind her. She turned to find a very irate Phoebe Perch seated in an armchair, tapping her foot. Maggie took a deep breath, crossed the room, and sat opposite her.

''All right, Miss Perch,'' she began. ''Let's set the ground rules. You don't like me and I don't much care for you. But you're going to answer my questions truthfully and to the best of your ability. Because if you don't, you will most probably be charged with suspicion of murder and spend several long weeks in the local jail—which I very much imagine is a dark iron holding cell with a drain in the floor for a bathroom—while you wait for the police investigation to close.''

Phoebe's jaw dropped. ''I-I ain't killed nobody!'' she stammered. Her hands suddenly twisted in her lap. At last, some of the old Phoebe, the original Phoebe—whatever low creature that had been—peeked through the veneer. ''You can't pin it on me!''

Maggie didn't give any sign that she had noticed the slip. ''When did you first meet Sam Warden?''

Phoebe was breathing quickly and heavily, her delicate nostrils fluttering. And then she seemed to collect herself, draw herself up. ''I never met him,'' she said, regathering her disdainful tone. ''The name means nothing to me.''

Maggie didn't let her expression change. She said, ''Doesn't it seem strange that he would ask you here, a complete stranger, when the intent was to murder you?''

Phoebe, completely recovered now, said, ''The man's obviously a lunatic. My invitation was from . . . another party entirely. It's just a mistake, that's all. And I ask you again, who are *you* to question *me*!''

''Stop fencing, Miss Perch. Changing the subject won't help. Where were you last night?''

The other woman's eyebrow furrowed. ''That's the most ridiculous question I have ever heard in my life! I was right here, asleep in my room. Which is drafty, by the way.'' She lifted her chin. ''I think I shall move.''

Maggie tried again. ''When and where did you first meet A. M. Andrews?''

Phoebe made a face. ''You are full to the brim with silly questions, Miss Maguire! I met him at the same time you did.''

Time for a new tack. ''Did you notice anything missing from the dinner table last night?''

Phoebe rolled her eyes. ''Why? Was he bludgeoned to

death with a biscuit? Really, I don't see the need to—''

''In particular,'' Maggie broke in, ''the carving knife?''

Phoebe's mouth opened in surprise, and just as quickly clicked closed. ''Why should I notice the carving knife? The ham was at the other end of the table.''

''And after we all left the game room? Did you notice anything then?''

Phoebe gave a little huff. ''As you recall, Miss Maguire, I fainted *in* the game room. Someone carried me upstairs.''

With a little smile that she had to force, Maggie said, ''Fainting seems like an extreme reaction from someone who's never heard of Sam Warden, don't you think?''

''It was a shock, that was all. Anyone would have been shocked. The threat could have come from . . . Saint Nicholas!''

Maggie sighed. She wasn't going to get any more out of Phoebe this morning. She rose and said, ''That will be all for now, Miss Perch. And don't change rooms.''

Phoebe stood up, spun on her heel and walked to the door, turning at the last moment. With a face that was pure cat, she said, ''I trust you and your 'cousin' will have a—''

''That's all, Miss Perch,'' said Maggie through clenched teeth. Digging nails into her palms, she watched as Phoebe slammed the door behind her. It had taken every ounce on self-control she had not to slap the woman. She wanted to throw her knives. Preferably at a large poster of Phoebe Perch.

The door creaked open, and Grady stuck his head through the opening. ''Safe to come in?''

''Just barely,'' Maggie snarled. ''That woman is the definition of obnoxious.''

Grady smiled and let himself in. ''I hope that's not a prophecy.'' He dug into his pocket. ''I found her invitation. Unfortunately, she tore it up.'' His hand appeared again, filled with tiny scraps of ivory parchment. ''Fortunately for us, she forgot that there isn't any maid service. I'll paste it together later.''

Maggie nodded her head as he tucked the scraps into his pocket again. "She go upstairs?"

"Like she was shot from a gun. The others are still waiting, though."

"Any sign of Gus yet?"

Grady gave his head a shake. "No. You know, something bothers me about Gus. I've got this nagging feeling that I've seen him before."

Maggie tilted her head. She said, "You, too? I just can't get a firm grip on it. Didn't even strike me until last night. I thought maybe he just reminded me of somebody else. But there's something . . ." Maggie let the sentence trail off, and stared into the space over Grady's shoulder.

"Mags? You want Mercury next?"

"What? No. Roman Kellogg, I think."

Grady took off his glasses and pulled out his handkerchief. "I overheard something last night. In the hall."

Maggie arched her brows. "And you didn't tell me?"

"Well, I *planned* to," he said, holding his spectacles up to the light with a frown. He was being theatrical again. Maggie waited.

"All that anagram business pushed it out of my brain," he continued, finally. "Want to hear it now?"

"No," she said. "I want to hear it a week from Thursday. Of *course* I want to hear it now!"

He rubbed at the glasses some more, while he quoted word for word—and with greater than average dramatic skill, Maggie thought—the Kelloggs' conversation.

"So Roman Kellogg lifted Warden's life—or parts thereof—and turned them into this character, Salty Bob. Temperance does the writing, and under duress, it would seem. Good, Grady. That gives me a place to start."

"Well, while you start, I believe I'll go see if I can dig up Gus. Oh, dear. Bad choice of words."

Maggie smiled. "Get going."

• • •

"How did you know about that?" growled Roman Kellogg. If Maggie wasn't mistaken, he was about two jumps away from coming out of that chair and throttling her. For a moment, she wished she'd asked Grady to stay.

She decided to brave it out. She leaned forward, hoping to intimidate him. "That doesn't really matter, does it, Mr. Kellogg? That fact is that Sam Warden does have a reason to kill you—slim, I'll admit, but a reason. And you lied about it. As I recall, you said you'd never heard of him."

Kellogg came out of his chair in a rush and Maggie instinctively reached for his arm. She'd have him in a hold and flat on his back before he knew what hit him.

But he didn't charge her. Instead, he immediately turned about and headed straight for the liquor cabinet, leaving Maggie hunched with her arms outstretched, and feeling very foolish indeed.

Fortunately, he didn't see her. She flopped back into her chair, rolling her eyes at her mistake while Kellogg fixed himself a whiskey and soda. He took a long drink, then turned toward her, his glass half-drained.

"All right," he said, wiping his mouth with the back of his free hand. "You're clever. Happy?"

"I'd be happier if you'd tell me when those demands started, and when they stopped."

His eyes narrowed. "They stopped a few years ago. Maybe five. And they lasted a year, off and on. I thought he went to prison. Then I heard he drowned. Glad to be rid of the sonofabitch."

Maggie sat up a little straighter. "I'll let that profanity pass, Mr. Kellogg. Did you ever meet Sam Warden?"

"No." He took another drink. Smaller, this time.

"Has your wife met him?"

He frowned. "That's a stupid question. Of course not. I'd know."

"How long have the two of you been married?"

"I don't see what business it is of yours. But if you must

know, nineteen years.'' He took a last sip, then put his glass down.

''And you've been writing all that time? Writing books, I mean?''

Kellogg pulled himself up a little straighter. ''For the past fifteen years. Thirty-six titles.''

''And has your wife been writing them exclusively all that time?''

Kellogg's eyes flashed dark. ''What? How dare you insinuate—''

''I am insinuating nothing, Mr. Kellogg.'' Maggie tensed. If he did charge her, she'd be ready. ''It's merely a fact. I asked you—very politely, I thought—just how long it has been a fact.''

Kellogg's hands clenched into fists, and his face, already ruddy, was working its way to beet-red. ''I don't have to answer that.''

Maggie stood up and, trying to reek confidence from every pore, went to the door. Her hand on the latch, she said, ''I believe you already have, Mr. Kellogg.''

He stormed past her, pushing the door open and thundering through the dining room. She heard him cross the lobby and slam the front door.

She looked after him. That little scene had been just a tad too close for comfort. The next time she'd have Grady stay in the room.

Or at least the building.

She turned toward the others, who were still huddled around the breakfast table, also watching after Roman Kellogg. Poor Temperance looked terror stricken. Well, best get it over with.

''Mrs. Kellogg?'' she said, in the kindest tone she could muster. ''Temperance, would you come this way, please?''

THIRTEEN

GRADY FOUGHT HIS WAY THROUGH ANOTHER PINE bough, and once on the other side, consulted the map of the island again. The Tropical Isle Trail had proved fruitless, although he had to admit the madrona trees on the other side of the island were quite picturesque. At least, he thought they were madrona trees. His map was for visitors, printed (complete with commentary) in two colors, and he'd found it in the lobby. But after walking four or five miles, he decided to cut from the Tropical Isle Trail over to the Majestic View Trail.

On the map the distance had appeared very small. After all, he was nearly back to the place where the paths separated when he cut off the first trail. But for the last half hour he'd been telling himself that it was just on the other side of the next tree. *Humph!*

He folded the map again and stuck it in his breast pocket, brushed a few pine needles from his coat, and squared his shoulders. He'd give it just three more trees, and then he was, by God, turning around. Let Maggie look for Gus herself, if he wasn't already back at the lodge.

But he came out into the open—and upon the Majestic View Trail—on the other side of the second tree. In fact, he had walked his way clear of the woods entirely. For a goodly distance in front of him, the land on one side of the trail was rolling and clear cut, deep in tall green grass and wildflowers and butterflies. A lone stag stood at alert on the crest of a hill, scented the air, then bolted. With two bounds, he was down in the valley. Four more, and he was out of sight.

Grady sighed. This was more like it. At least a fellow could see where he was going. And then he saw what had spooked the buck. Gus Thorpe, walking over the hill.

Grady waved, but Gus didn't see him. After all, he could barely see Gus, who was coming down the trail from the "majestic view" it promised. He decided to wait, and then he remembered about Andrews, and was suddenly glad Gus hadn't seen him. If Gus was the perpetrator, he just might take it into his head to scoot into the trees. A man like that could probably evade detection on an island like this for years.

So Grady pulled out his pistol, made sure there was a cartridge in the chamber and stuck it nearer his hand, in his coat pocket. And he waited.

Maggie, meanwhile, was carefully searching Andrews's room, mindless of the corpse on the bed. She'd long ago gotten used to bodies, and they didn't generally bother her. Well, not after they were covered with a sheet, as was Mr. Andrews. The sheet tented on the knife's blade—still stuck in his chest, its grip jutting high—so it didn't even look like a body, not really. It smelled like one, though. Maggie had thrown open the window first thing.

The rest of the interviews had proved the same as useless. Temperance Kellogg fainted at the first suggestion that she, alone, might be writing the Mesa Mike books, and Mercury had had nothing to add to what he'd told them last night. Carlisle was still in his room. And Mrs. Friar—when she came to—proved to be a dead end as well, being primarily interested in when Maggie would let them move the body to the cellar. Stains on the mattress, you know.

So here she was. She'd already gone through Andrews's wardrobe and all the suit and pants and jacket pockets therein, and now she was sifting carefully through Andrews's bureau drawers and wishing the stink would lift a little. Not of the body, per se. That hadn't begun yet. This stink arose from . . . Well, Mr. Andrews, like all murder victims—like all recently deceased people—had, as his last act, lost control of all his voluntary muscles. He'd wet himself, and worse.

As Maggie pulled out the final drawer, she thought again how, in death, we all returned to the cradle and soiled our nappies. It was God's way of cutting us down to size.

She wondered if a clothespin on her nose would help.

And then, beneath a small stack of shirts, she found something interesting. A wallet. Not that a wallet in itself was so amazing. What made it interesting was that it was the *second* wallet. She'd already found one belonging to Andrews in the top drawer.

She pulled the second wallet out and opened it. She shook her head and looked again at the card. " 'Humbert J. Thackery,' " she read aloud. " 'Master Tragedian.' "

She turned around and looked at the body. "Thackery? Humbert J. Thackery?" she asked the inert form.

She went back to the wallet again. Seven more calling cards, the same as the first. There was a good bit of money—nearly three hundred dollars—and an identification pass from the Roxie's Elite Bijou Theater in Denver, also made out in the name of Humbert Thackery. In the back, she found a battered photograph of a company of actors in costume, with a younger Humbert J. Thackery (a.k.a. Andrews) at center stage and a banner overhead that read QUINN AND BUMBRIDGE THEATER—NEW YORK CITY And a brass token from someplace called Kitty's Kat House, in Denver, which had a figure of a scantily clad woman on one side and the words *Good for One All Night Regular or One De-Luxe Special* engraved upon the reverse.

She stuck the token back in, deciding not to dwell upon what they meant by "One De-Luxe Special," and searched the rest of the drawer. She found nothing, and stood up, knees creaking. Still clutching the wallet, she went to the door and opened it a crack, then sat down in the chair Rance Carlisle had collapsed into earlier that morning.

"Humbert J. Thackery," she said. "An actor. Not A. M. Andrews at all. Not Sam Warden." She stared at the bed for a moment, her brow creasing. "Suds. Hired by Sam Warden? Or were you invited, like everybody else?"

The sheeted corpse gave no answer.

Grady stood up and waved. Gus broke out in a grin and waved back. "Went up to see what the Sam Hill a 'Majestic View' looked like," Gus called as he neared. "It's purty, all right, but I've seen better. And I damn near crippled myself."

Grady laughed, and eased his hand away from his pocket. "I know how you feel, Gus. I went down the Tropical Isle Trail first."

Gus drew even with him, and they started back toward the lodge. "Reckon I spend too much time on my horse," Gus said. "Ain't got no walkin' muscles. Saw a couple'a deer, though. One was a twelve point buck."

Grady opened his mouth to say he'd seen the buck, too, then thought better of it. Best not to let Gus know he'd been waiting for him. He might not take kindly to his having lain in wait, so to speak.

He said, "Quite a hubbub at the lodge this morning."

Gus shrugged. "They mad cause I left a'fore breakfast? Swiped a couple'a rolls off the table. Sure hope they ain't mad about a little thing like that."

"No," said Grady, as they walked along. "Nothing of the kind. It's Mr. Andrews."

Gus pursed his lips for a second. "He that uppity fella in the patched suit? The one who wants to bag him an elk?"

Grady nodded.

"Dumbest thing I ever heard. Why, he says best time

for elk huntin' is the early mornin'. I've brought down elk mornin', noon, and night. Betwixt you and me, I don't think that boy knows squat about huntin'." Gus made a face. "Goldurn, but my calves are about to kill me! They got any ridin' horses around? All I seen was a buggy. I ain't gonna make this walk again."

Grady said, "Gus—"

"No, I'll be all stove up and soakin' my extremities in a liniment bath, that's what I'll be doin'. You say somethin', Grady?"

Getting Gus to talk was hard, but getting him to shut up was harder. Grady said, "It's about Mr. Andrews, Gus. This morning, my cousin and I found him. He's been murdered."

Grady walked on a few steps before he realized that Gus was no longer beside him. He whirled around, thinking that Gus had taken off at a run, but found him, three steps back, sitting on the ground.

"Gus? Are you all right?"

Gus swallowed hard, then looked up. "M-murdered? All the way *dead*?"

Grady nodded.

"I sure am sorry I said them things, Grady. I take 'em all back." He shook his head sorrowfully. "How'd they do him in?"

"A knife."

Gus gripped his head with his hands for a moment. "A knife. I'd a lot rather be shot, myself. Quick and you don't hardly know it's comin'." He seemed to consider it for a second and added, " 'Course, I'd prefer either one to hangin'. I seen one boy dangle most of a half hour before he was clear dead."

Grady helped him to his feet. "You seen a lot of men hanged, have you?"

They started walking again.

"Three. Two of 'em, I hanged myself. Well, more like I was a party to it. They was rustlers. Rustlers is a good bit different than a suit-wearin' man on vacation.''

Well, he had a point there. The two walked on in silence for a bit, Gus seeming to ponder Andrews's death, and Grady deciding what to do next. What would Maggie want him to do? At last, he decided that whether she liked it or not, it was best to strike while the iron was hot.

He said, ''Gus, when did you meet Sam Warden?''

The small man didn't break stride. ''Reckoned you'd be askin' again. Suppose I'd better fess up. I ain't no good at keepin' a secret nohow. Back about eighteen-and-seventy-two, he bilked a friend'a mine, bilked him bad. Poor old coot. Warden got all his savings. Y'know, cowhands ain't got much, but he'd put by about seven hundred dollars over the years. That's a powerful lot of money. It was for when he died, for his daughter, back East. Anyways, he was so shamed and sorrowful about lettin' Warden take him, he up and shot himself right through the head.''

Grady missed a step, but Gus just kept walking, his expression stoic. ''Got me so fired up that I rode about sixty miles, till I tracked that sidewinder down. I roped and hog-tied him, and hauled him back to Sweetwater. I turned him over to the law and sent the reward to Peggy, back East. That was ol' Gus's little girl. Well, I reckon she was about thirty by that time.''

Gus scratched the back of his neck. ''The thing was, Warden skipped out. Oh, he was tried and sentenced, the whole thing real legal, but he hopped off the prison wagon. Killed a couple'a guards, and word was he was a'comin' for me next. So I changed my name and took work at another ranch. I used to be Billy Small. I took ol' Gus's name to whatchacall . . . Honor him, I guess.''

Grady said, ''Would you know him if you saw him again?''

Gus reached into his pocket, drew out his tobacco pouch and eased it open. ''Grady, when I hog-tied him and hauled him back to Sweetwater, he was five-foot-eleven with hair and a mustache darker'n the inside of a black hog at midnight, and a beak you could hang your duster on.'' He finished rolling the smoke, gave it a quick lick, and stuck it in his mouth.

''I heard tell,'' Gus said, striking a match, ''that when they carted him to prison, he was pug-nosed, blond, and five-foot-nine.'' He lit his smoke, then waved the match out. ''Hell,'' he said, as he tossed the match to the ground. ''I wouldn't know Sam Warden if he was pissin' on my boots.''

FOURTEEN

MAGGIE AND GRADY WERE UPSTAIRS IN MAGGIE'S room. Grady had just finished relating Gus Thorpe's story.

"On one hand, it sounds perfectly straight," Maggie said. Grady picked up Andrews's—that was to say, Humbert J. Thackery's—wallet, and leafed through it.

Even though Grady didn't seem to be paying her much mind, Maggie continued, "Quite similar to Mercury's tale of woe, in fact. Here Gus was, a perfectly upstanding citizen who did his duty, and now Warden is on his trail for a crime that wasn't a crime. On the other hand, I *still* say I've seen him someplacc before. And I agree that he did an excellent job of keeping his identity secret. As well as the fact of his having known Warden."

Grady, rifled through Andrews's wallet again. "Did you ever stop to wonder?" he mused. "I mean, maybe Andrews was invited here, just like the rest of us. Maybe he was traveling under another name." He looked up. "Maybe he changed it. Maybe he really *was* in business in Portland. Former actors have been known to do such things, you know. I mean, change their names. Show people don't exactly fit into the main of society."

He'd done it again: sidetracked her. With annoyance, she snapped, "Were you listening to a word I said?" Then she sighed, and just gave in to it. You couldn't fight Grady. He was a force of nature.

"That doesn't explain why his name is an anagram for Sam Warden," she said. "I've thought about it. I think somebody—probably Warden himself—hired Andrews or Thackery or whatever his real name was to come here and impersonate him."

"But how do you know it was Warden who hired him?" Grady asked, and she knew he was about to be extremely annoying. "How do you know it wasn't somebody else? Somebody who was Warden's friend or business partner or whatever? May I remind you that for all we know, Warden's at the bottom of the bay. And there still exists the possibility that we're not the only people on this island."

Her mouth set, Maggie stood up and went to the window. Grady was chock-full of speculations that complicated things far too much and pulled her off the track.

But what if one of Grady's theories was right?

Below, down by the horseshoe cove, two people were standing on the beach. Phoebe Perch and Temperance Kellogg, of all people. If she'd worked at it day and night for a week, she couldn't have come up with two women more unlikely to be develop a friendship—not even the social, passing kind.

Still puzzling over the two women, who seemed to be deep in conversation, Maggie said, "You know, I could think a great deal better if someone were paying me."

She glanced round in time to see Grady lounging back on the bed, making himself at home. As usual. Smiling, he closed his eyes.

Maggie turned back to the window. These two women were still in exactly the same place, still talking. She said, "You get Phoebe's invitation pasted back together yet?"

Behind her, Grady said, "And just when was I supposed to do this? While I was running all over the island looking for Gus? And, I might add, very nearly ruining my new suit. Which I wore for Mr. Edison."

Edison again. He'd just keep rubbing it in with a wire brush until he got tired of it. She wondered why he didn't go ask Mrs. Friar for a little rock salt to throw into the mix. She said, "All right. When you have time."

"Mags?"

She turned her back on the window. "What?"

"I don't remember you telling me you talked to Carlisle."

She sat down in an armchair. "Still in his room."

Grady cracked open one eye. "You sure?"

"I peeked in," she answered. "His drapes were pulled, but I could see him in bed."

"Sorry. No need to get huffy."

Maggie sat forward. "Huffy? I certainly am not huffy! Am I?"

The bulk of her conversation with Phoebe Perch concluded, Temperance Kellogg prepared to leave. "Well then, I'll be getting back," she said, and shifted her parasol to the other shoulder. She consulted her watch pin. "It's almost eleven-thirty, and Roman will be wanting—"

"Hang your Roman," said Phoebe, staring out over the swimming cove. "You never should have married that horse's backside, Mrs. Kellogg. You could have done so much better. I did. Oh, doesn't the water look scrumptious? See?" she said, pointing. "The shape of the cove and those net things break the waves. It's practically like glass. Not aquamarine, exactly. Would you say teal?"

"Mrs. Perch, let's go."

But Phoebe took a few short steps down to the edge of the water, and bent down, dipping her fingers. "Oh," she said, "it's absolutely perfect. Let's go wading!" Kneeling in the sand, she began to tug at the buttons on her shoes with manicured fingers.

But she stopped abruptly when a scream, distant and shrill, broke the stillness. She saw Temperance Kellogg staring up at the lodge, frozen in place as Mrs. Friar, a white-apronned speck, collapsed to the ground.

Phoebe stood up and took Temperance's arm. "Don't you faint on me," she commanded as they started up the hill.

Maggie ran out the front door just in time to meet Temperance Kellogg and Phoebe Perch, who were racing up from the cove as fast as their skirts would let them, and nearly tripped over Mrs. Friar.

"Is she all right?" Temperance asked, her voice trembling, as Maggie knelt to the body.

Maggie didn't see any blood. She pressed her fingers to the side of the housekeeper's throat.

"She's alive," Maggie announced. "Who screamed?"

"She did." Phoebe and Temperance answered as one.

"And there's the reason," announced Grady, who'd come down the porch steps right behind Maggie.

She looked up at him and followed his gaze. At first she saw nothing and glanced at Grady curiously.

"Stand up," he said.

She did, and then she saw it. A crumpled figure far away on the lawn, a few feet away from the edge of the woods. A man—with an axe handle jutting from his back.

Mrs. Friar moaned slightly.

Maggie glanced down, then up again at Temperance and Phoebe. They were both staring at the figure of the dead man. Temperance was white-faced and horrified. Maggie couldn't read Phoebe's expression.

"Mrs. Perch?" Maggie said. "Would you please help Mrs. Friar into the lodge?"

Before Phoebe had a chance to say that she certainly wasn't going to touch a *servant*, or some sentiment equally distasteful, Maggie said, "Grady?" and started down the grassy slope, toward the body.

"Well, he's dead." Maggie rose to her feet and brushed grass from her skirts thoughtfully.

"I could have told you that from the front porch," said Grady. He was off to the side—Grady had never been one for dead bodies—and staring toward the woods. He turned toward her. "Which one is it?"

Maggie sighed. "Roman Kellogg. You know, somebody shoved this axe in his back with quite a bit of force. I don't think it was thrown." Again, she studied the handle, the depth the blade had sunk in. It was not in his spine—he couldn't have stumbled out of the woods if it had severed his spine—but just to the side. It had gone through his ribs, cutting through them like a hot knife through paraffin, and into the vital organs.

"I think he was with somebody he trusted," she continued, "and he turned his back. I doubt anybody could have crept up on him in those woods. Too many crackly things underfoot."

Grady had taken a few steps toward the trees, his eyes were fixed on the ground. "They were in the woods, all right," he said. "By the tracks through the grass, it looks like old Roman came out alone." He knelt down, balancing on the balls of his feet. "What now?"

Maggie pressed a finger to her chin. The murderer would have hot-footed it back to the lodge. He'd probably gone through the trees and around the back, and entered through one of the back doors.

She said, "Go back into the forest and see if you can find anything. Site of the scuffle, if there was any."

"Right," said Grady, and started off. Then he paused and turned toward her. "You going to tell Mrs. Kellogg?"

Maggie nodded. "I think she already knows."

She started up the slope toward the lodge. Temperance Kellogg had everything to gain at the death of her husband. At last, there'd be an end to the bullying. And, from what she'd inferred from the interview with the late Roman Kellogg, and what Grady had told her, Temperance's income wouldn't suffer. She was perfectly capable of carrying on the Mesa Mike books all by herself.

Of course, there was the question of love. People loved the oddest people sometimes. Some women adored men who beat them, who lied to them, who cheated on them. She'd seen it time and time again. Some things were beyond understanding, and as she gained the porch steps and started up them, she was shaking her head in disgust.

Any man who raised a hand to Maggie Maguire would find himself in the next county before he could blink twice.

When she entered the lobby, still mulling over the fallibilities of womankind, the ladies were waiting. Mrs. Friar had revived and was sucking at a glass of water with the side of her face that worked. Temperance Kellogg was seated, looking as Maggie had last seen her: white as the proverbial ghost. Phoebe just appeared bored.

Before Maggie had a chance to speak, Phoebe said, "Well? Who is it? Or should I ask, who *was* it? Mrs. Kellogg is convinced it was her husband."

Temperance looked up. Tearless, Maggie noted, but obviously in great distress. Her voice thin and breaking, Temperance said, "I saw his suit. His brown country suit. It was him, wasn't it, Miss Maguire?"

Maggie went to the woman and, kneeling, placed a comforting hand on her shoulder. "I'm afraid it was, Mrs. Kellogg," she said gently. "I'm so sorry."

Temperance let out a wail that startled them all. "Oh, Roman!" she cried, and collapsed into tears.

"There, there," whispered Maggie—quite ineffectually, for Temperance just kept crying—and took the woman in her arms. "Now, now," she tried again. She supposed that this was not the moment to point out Roman's many shortcomings.

"Roman," sobbed Temperance. "Mr. Andrews, and now Roman! Oh, poor Mr. Andrews!"

"Mr. Andrews?" she heard Mrs. Friar mutter.

Maggie disentangled herself from Temperance and stood up. Turning toward Phoebe, she said, "Mrs. Perch, if you wouldn't mind helping Mrs. Kellogg to her room?"

Phoebe started to give her one of those exasperated looks, but Maggie ignored it, adding quickly, "Even if you *would* mind. Now, please."

As Phoebe—who didn't even pretend to be pleased—helped Temperance to her feet, Maggie turned toward Mrs. Friar. "Why did you say that?"

The housekeeper, her ruined face set, said, "Why did I say what?"

" 'Mr. Andrews.' "

The housekeeper frowned. "Well, her husband's just took an axe in the back! If that was me, I wouldn't be thinkin' about some man I hardly knew, even if he did go and get himself killed just this morning."

Maggie agreed, but said nothing except, "I see. Why did you scream?"

Mrs. Friar raised one eyebrow. "Did I? Well, I suppose I might've. When he keeled over. I saw somebody come staggerin' out of the woods, down by that grandaddy of a fir tree. Well, he wasn't staggerin' at first. Took the first couple of steps okay, I guess. But then he started weavin' and lurchin', and pretty soon he just fell over. I saw the handle stickin' out of his back, and I just knew."

"Knew?"

Mrs. Friar looked at her in disgust. "Knew that he was dead. What did you think?"

"What's wrong with Mrs. Kellogg?" asked a male voice from the staircase. Mercury. He was coming down the stairs, but staring up them, over his shoulder. He turned toward Maggie. "Is it lunchtime yet?"

FIFTEEN

MRS. FRIAR WAS SUFFICIENTLY RECOVERED TO PREpare lunch, and went off to the kitchen. Maggie sent Mercury to wait in the dining room, then went upstairs to find Gus and Rance Carlisle. She found Rance snoring in his shadowy room and woke him.

"And what, in the name of thunder, are you doing in here?" he roared, coming out of sleep. Then his expression changed from one of annoyance to one more predatory. Softly, and slick as butter, he said, "What *are* you doing in my room, Miss Maguire?" And winked.

Maggie crossed her arms. "Come downstairs, Mr. Carlisle."

"Rance," he said, hoisting himself up to sit with his back against the headboard, smiling. "Just call me Rance, sweet pea."

Rankled, Maggie said, "There's been another murder, *Mr.* Carlisle," and underscored the Mister. "Downstairs, in the dining room. If you wouldn't mind."

His smile broadened. "And what if I do?"

Maggie pursed her lips. "Mr. Carlisle, I am extremely close to flinging you out the door. Don't press me." She strode over to his windows and pulled the heavy curtains.

Light flooded the room, revealing Carlisle in his nightshirt, squinting against the glare. "Now, what did you have to go and do that for, woman?" he said, blinking.

"Downstairs," Maggie said on her way out the door. "Fifteen minutes."

"Hey!" she heard Carlisle call after her. "Did you say somebody else got himself murdered?"

She didn't answer. When she'd pulled back the curtains, she'd seen Grady coming out of the woods. He wasn't alone.

"Mr. Kellogg? Murdered? Well, if that ain't the gol-darnedest thing!" Gus poked his hat back with a thumb and shook his head.

Grady kept walking—a half step behind Gus, just in case. He'd found him in the woods. Oh, he'd been coming from the other direction, all right, but that could easily have been a ruse. Said he'd been "just pokin' around."

Grady said, "It's not so amazing. Warden said he was going to kill us all. You heard the Edison. I'm only surprised that we're not falling faster."

They were almost to the lodge, having passed the barn and paddocks. Gus stopped. Grady, for a fleeting moment, thought, *He's got a gun, he's going to turn and shoot me like a dog.* But then Gus turned toward him, empty-handed, and remarked, "They got some decent ridin' horses in there. I might maybe saddle one up if I got another hanker to sight-see."

Grady kept walking, this time with his eyes on the ground. He could have been safely at home, moping and staring at the walls, instead of finding bodies at every turn. Damn that Maggie, anyway!

Gus said, "Well, two before lunch," and Grady had to regroup his thoughts quickly.

"Murders, you mean?" Forget Maggie and concentrate on the killings.

Gus continued, "Seems a powerful lot to me. Grady, you all right?"

"Yes. Yes, I'm fine. I—"

"There you are!" Maggie was walking toward them,

over the lawn, smiling. "Mrs. Friar's thrown some lunch together."

Gus turned toward her. "You'll excuse me for sayin' it, Miss, but it beats me how you can smile at a time like this. Mr. Kellogg being dead and all, and killed in a yellow-livered way, too, from what Grady said."

Maggie held on to her smile. She said, "And where were you at the time of the killing, Gus?"

Without missing a beat, Gus said, "Yonder," and pointed toward the trees in the opposite direction from where the unfortunate Roman Kellogg had met his maker. "I already told Grady." And then, with just an edge of accusation in his voice, he asked, "Where were you, Miss?"

Grady covered his mouth quickly, and the laugh emerged as a muffled cough.

Maggie's brows knit, then relaxed. "In the lobby, Gus. With Grady." She turned toward her cousin. Quickly, he lowered his hand.

In that pleasant, even tone that he knew was the next thing away from an hour's target tossing with blades (thank God she hadn't brought them—the damages in a place like this would likely cost a half year's salary) she said, "If you wouldn't mind, would you carry the body up before you come in to lunch?" She waved toward an open cellar door. "Mrs. Friar opened up the root cellar for you. Put him in there."

Then she turned on her heel and started back toward the lodge, skirts swishing.

Gus took his hat all the way off and scratched at his head. "You reckon she meant me, too?"

Grady's scowl was directed at life in general, particularly the part of it that had a fellow rescuing Thomas Edison one minute and surrounded by corpses in the company of a possible murderer the next.

To Gus, he said, "Come on."

• • •

They had the body halfway to the front of the lodge—Kellogg had been an imposing man in life, but in death, he was heavier than a solid lead wagon. Without the wheels. Grady dropped his end first—he had the corpse by the arms—and mopped his brow with a handkerchief.

Little Gus, who seemed a good bit stronger than his size would have indicated, dropped Kellogg's feet and plopped on the ground. Reaching into his pocket for his fixings, he said, "When we started out, I ain't ashamed to say I was halfway to cryin' on account of his been killed so heinous. But, tarnation, Mr. Kellogg's a weighty sonofabitch! Now I'm just looking at him like a load'a grain what's got to be moved all at once."

He gave his cigarette a last lick, then paused, reconsidering the corpse. "Don't s'pose we could take that hatchet outta his back, could we? Don't seem right, just leavin' it there."

Grady sat down, too, and stuck his handkerchief in his pocket. "She didn't say, so I wouldn't touch it if I were you."

Actually, if you managed not to look at the body, it was rather peaceful just sitting on the lawn. From where they were, the cove looked blue as wedgewood and glassy, shimmering slightly in the sunlight. A few gulls swooped low, looking for food. They came up empty-beaked, and circled high up, on the currents. Charming.

The banging of the screen door diverted his attention. It was Phoebe Perch. She came down the steps in that bizarre apparel only women would have the nerve to actually try to swim in. Covered from head to toe in black, ruffled and pleated and carrying at least three beach towels over her arm, she came down the steps. Grady caught her eye, but she pointed her nose in the air—perhaps it was the body, perhaps it was him—and marched toward the cove.

"She sure is stuck-up," said Gus, around his smoldering cigarette.

"Yes," said Grady. "She is that, all right. Ready for another go?"

Gus creaked to his feet and stepped on the remains of his smoke. "Reckon."

The two men had the late Mr. Kellogg even with the front porch when Gus dropped his end. He held up a hand. "Hold up," he said. "My back's about to give out. Wish somebody'd kept this fat bastard from eatin' so much taters and sweets while he was livin'."

Grady had let his end go, too, and walked over to sit on the steps. The handkerchief came out and he worked it over his face and neck, saying, "He's coming up in the world. A few minutes ago, he was just a sonofabitch. Or a load of oats or something."

"Well . . ." Gus started toward the steps.

Grady polished the sweat off his glasses, then put his handkerchief away. From this angle, he had a much better view of the tennis and badminton courts. Didn't look like he'd get to play now, though. Wouldn't really be proper, he supposed. The view of the cove was much better, though. He could see Phoebe Perch, that paragon of virtue, out in the water. She was performing the backstroke, he believed. The cove was bigger than he'd thought—in it, she was like a gnat in a soup bowl.

Gus sagged down beside him, his knees popping. When Grady looked from his knees to his face, Gus said, "A few years of workin' around cattle and green-broke horses test a man's bones."

Grady nodded.

Voices drifted out the front door. No complete sentences, just snatches of sound. Maggie's voice, raised. Carlisle's voice, also raised. Well, when *wasn't* Carlisle's voice raised, the big blustering windbag.

"One more haul ought to get him to the root cellar," said Grady, pointing at the body. He'd be glad to have Mr. Kellogg out of sight. He didn't mean to seem cruel, but that axe sticking out of his back gave him the willies. At least the body hadn't started to stiffen, yet.

There. Something to be thankful for.

Gus stood up, facing the lodge with a worried expression on his face. "You reckon they've already et?"

"I'm sure they saved—" Grady stopped. He stared toward the cove to see Phoebe Perch bob under the water. He waited for her to resurface, but she came up about twenty feet from where she'd gone down. The water about her darkened sickly, and then, arms flailing, she began to swiftly—too swiftly—move backward through the water.

"Maggie!" he cried. "Maggie, come now!" And leaving Gus and the body behind, sprinted down the slope toward the cove.

SIXTEEN

MAGGIE STOPPED HER ARGUMENT WITH RANCE Carlisle midsentence when she heard Grady. She bolted for the door and was outside in three seconds, jumping off the porch steps and over Gus and running down the lawn.

The moment she saw the cove and Grady thundering toward it, saw Phoebe being dragged like a ragdoll through the stained water, she knew with a sick certainty what was happening.

Even as she sprinted toward the beach, she shouted, "Grady! Grady, no! Don't!"

He couldn't hear her. He had his jacket off already—she nearly tripped over it—and was at the water line, jerking off one shoe, then the next.

Cursing her skirts, she put on a burst of speed, gave a leap, and caught him, the water halfway up their thighs.

"Get out!" she screamed, on the edge of hysterics.

"But Miss Perch is—"

This time she didn't scream. She fell back on instinct and clipped him sharply on the back of his head, and even as he crumpled she began hauling him out of the water. The struggle had taken her in farther, and the water was halfway to her waist. Panic beating at her, she pulled him backward, her skirts weighted like so much concrete. By the time she dragged him to the shore, she was crying.

Mercury, the first guest on the scene, had taken one look at the water, and was kneeling about twenty feet away, vomiting into the grass. Next, she was aware of Rance Carlisle. He stood behind her, saying, "Dear God," over and over.

The panic under control, pushed away, Maggie took a quick wipe at her eyes and patted Grady's cheek. He didn't come to, and gingerly, she felt for his pulse. It was strong, thank goodness. Wouldn't do at all to kill him in the name of saving him.

"Dear God," said Rance Carlisle again, and sat down in the sand next to her. His breath was short, and he fumbled in his pocket before he pulled out his small vial of pills. Popping one under his tongue, he said, "I've never . . . never seen . . ."

Mercury, green-faced, walked up just as Grady groaned. "Good boy," Maggie muttered, and held a hand up to Mercury. Her skirts weighed a ton, and if all these men hadn't been around, she would have just as soon stripped them off.

Mercury helped her up, dripping and heavy as a horse, just in time to see Phoebe's lifeless torso upend momentarily. That was all there was, just a torso, severed at the waist and ending in jagged bone and strings of tissue.

A half second later, almost too quick for the eye to catch, a dorsal fin emerged to cut the water. Phoebe's torso was jerked from sight. A moment later, it came up again. Minus the head.

"Jesus," Mercury breathed. He'd gone pale, almost ashy, and he wavered on his feet.

"No," said Maggie. "He didn't have a thing to do with this." She turned away from the water and looked down at Grady. He was awake, grimacing and feeling the back of his neck. To Mercury, she said, "Mercury? Mercury, snap out of it. Help me get him back to the lodge."

Grady between them and Rance trailing behind, they made their way up the slope. Mrs. Friar and Gus—and the late Roman Kellogg—were waiting for them. Gus's face was drained of blood and he held his hat over his chest.

Mrs. Friar was wringing her apron in her hands. When they came near, she blurted, "Miss Maguire, I swear I don't know what . . . that is, the net's supposed to keep sharks *out* of the cove. I don't know what . . . what . . ."

Maggie sank down on the steps. "It's all right, Mrs. Friar. It's not your fault." She picked up a handful of her skirt and wrung it out. Water cascaded down the steps. Getting upstairs to change was going to be a bit of a trick.

Wearily, she said, "Mercury?" He was staring at Roman Kellogg's corpse. He sat down hard on the edge of the steps, taking Grady down with him. Grady went all the way to the ground, and sat there, dazed and rubbing his neck. "Could you help Gus with Mr. Kellogg? Once you recover, I mean? Grady and Mr. Carlisle are in no condition."

Mercury nodded mutely and then, with what looked like a tremendous effort, walked over to Mr. Kellogg. Gingerly, he picked up the corpse's feet. "Um, Gus?" he said.

Maggie twisted the water out of another handful of skirt. "Mrs. Friar, why don't you go inside and sit down or something. You don't look well." Actually, it was hard to tell any difference, but Maggie just wanted to get all these people away from her. She wanted to go upstairs and lock herself in her room and just make it all *stop* for as long as possible. Also, she wanted to throw up.

She wrung more water from her skirts, then stood up. "Will you be all right, Mr. Carlisle?"

Red-faced, he nodded curtly.

"All right then, Grady?" He lifted his face. His eyes were still a little wobbly. Vacant, too. She held her hand down to him. "Up and at 'em," she said, adding when he staggered to his feet, "Come on, there's a good boy."

Slowly, she and Grady, each as unstable as the other, went into the lodge behind Mrs. Friar.

"Mommy?" said Grady, halfway up the stairs.

"That's right," soothed Maggie, hanging on to the balustrade for dear life with one hand, and Grady with the other. "Another step."

After depositing Grady in his room, Maggie trudged across the hall, closed the door behind her, and immediately took off her dress, corset, bustle, and petticoats. Wet drawers clinging to her legs, she carried the clothing into the bathroom and hung them up the best she could, then exchanged her soggy drawers and chemise for dry ones.

Next, she went to the one place the wall was free of paintings or mirrors or bric-a-brac or furniture, and faced it. Filling her cheeks with air, she blew it out with a *whoosh*. Then, crouching down, she put her head on the floor with her hands out, making a tripod, and shifted her weight, lifting her feet up and her backside overhead, until she was doing a handstand: her fanny and heels against the wall, straight up.

The Mystic Maharajah Rama (He Sleeps on a Bed of Nails and Pierces His Cheeks and Tongue with a Silver Spike!) had always told her that standing on one's head was the best way to think things out. Of course, she preferred knives, but she didn't happen to have any at the moment.

Now, what had Rama said, those many years ago? Clear your mind, that was it. Clear your mind, and the answer will come to you like a jewel on a lily pad.

After ten minutes, no lily pad—with or without jewel—had surfaced. Of course, it didn't help that she couldn't clear her mind. Who could, at a time like this? She'd never felt so blasted helpless!

She opened her eyes and stared at the upside-down room. First, she'd been certain that Warden was Mr. Andrews, but Andrews had been the first one killed, and the murders continued. But Mr. Andrews *wasn't* Mr. Andrews. Mr. Andrews was Mr. Humbert J. Thackery, Master Tragedian.

Probably.

Maybe.

Suddenly, she remembered that she hadn't had the body moved, and grimaced. She'd better put Grady and Mercury onto that before Andrews (or Thackery) started to get too ripe.

Then there was Mr. Kellogg. She hadn't really suspected him. She hadn't really liked him, either. Oh, all right, she found him a particularly odious man, and she was certain all the other guests—with the possible exception of his wife—agreed with her.

However, just because Roman Kellogg was a bully didn't justify someone sinking that axe blade into his back. And some stupid secondary character in his books—no, make that Temperance Kellogg's books—didn't make the killing seem worthwhile, either, not even for Sam Warden.

There had to be something else, some larger reason.

And poor Phoebe Perch! Such a tragic accident! But was it an accident? It had already occurred to her that someone—that someone being Sam Warden—might have deliberately let the shark in the cove before the guests had arrived on the island.

Her lips set into a hard line. If that were true, Sam Warden was even more despicable than she'd previously thought. And that was pretty damned despicable.

She thought of Pheobe Perch's severed torso again, bobbing like a macabre seaside toy in the water, and lost her balance. Suddenly going opposite directions, her right foot thudded against the wall. The left one came perilously close to the floor.

"Suds!" she grumbled softly, before kicking up again. There, legs against the wall. Nice and straight. Maybe she wasn't as calm and detached as she liked to imagine.

Think of something different.

There was something else, some remark Mrs. Friar had made, was it? Something . . . Blast! It was all so muddled!

There was a rap at the door and she stiffened, but then Grady's voice followed with a "Mags?" and she relaxed. Not just because it was him, but because if he knew who she was and how to find her, he must have recovered from that crack to the back of his head.

"Come in," she said. "Close the door behind you, please."

Grady entered, glanced at her without comment, then shut the door. He cocked an elbow over the bureau top and leaned against it. "Maggie dearest? You hit me, didn't you?"

She inched one of her hands to the side. Better. "Just as hard as I could. You were about to feed yourself to a shark."

When he didn't answer, she added, "You all right now?"

"Aside from the ringing in my ears and the triple vision, I'm all right. Well, I will be, once the migraine and tremors go away."

"Grady!"

He waved a hand. "Oh, don't get up. I'm teasing you. Not that you don't deserve it, Maggie. You hit me a fair clip out there. But thank you, I suppose, for saving me from a fool's errand."

Maggie tried to shrug, but lost her balance and this time, she came toppling down. Well, not toppling, precisely. She saved it at the last second, and landed neatly on her knees. *Ta Da!* she thought as she lifted her head and turned to sit against the wall, knees tucked under her chin, arms wrapped round them.

Grady, with no change of expression, said, "Has Quincy ever witnessed this little trick?"

A flush raced up Maggie's neck and heated her cheeks before she realized it. Drat that Grady, anyway, bringing Quin up at a time like this. Maggie opened her mouth, then thought better and snapped it shut.

"I thought not," said Grady, smugly. "And it's so entertaining with you in your underwear. I think you should show him the minute we get back. If we get back."

"Unless you've got something useful to say," she

growled, "go away. Play with the Edison or something."

"Tut-tut. I've got something to show you."

She raised a brow, happy to leave the subject of Quincy Applegate behind. "What?"

"Remember that invitation you asked me to glue—"

"You put it together?" said Maggie, springing to her feet in one bound. "Let me see!"

She started toward him, but Grady held up his hands. "You think I could glue together that jigsawed mess in a half hour?" He looked her up and down. "I only got part of it, but I think it's the important part. And put on a dress, please? It's rather disconcerting, you know, you running around in your underwear. After all, Maggie, I'm a single man. I'm not used to such immodest goings-on."

She thought of Miriam and Jane and Cleo and Beth Ann and Patience and so on—she could recite the list for days—plus all the girls from the Barbary Coast she hadn't known about. She said, "Grady, I think I can say with assurance that you're the *least* unseasoned man I know. Married or unmarried. Now let me see that invitation."

Grady made a face at her, but dipped two fingers into his breast pocket and drew out a jagged, mosaic-like strip. He handed it to her, saying, "Careful."

Cautiously, she took it from him. He was right. It was the important part, although not nearly so important as she had once thought it to be. It said: *Mr. John B. Scofield requests the*

"So," said Maggie. "Johnny Scofield. Heir to the Scofield silver fortune. My, my. Our Phoebe set her sights high, didn't she?"

Grady nodded. "Indeed, rest her soul. Now the dress?"

"Dress? Oh." Maggie handed back the scrap of invitation and walked to the wardrobe. "Just a minute," she said, sorting through it until her hand landed on a rather somber, dark blue frock. Well, there had been three deaths in one day. A pity she hadn't brought black.

She draped the dress over her arms, scooped up two

folded petticoats from the bottom shelf, and headed for the bathroom. "I'll be with you in a shake," she said, and closed the door behind her.

"Mind if I wait?" Grady called.

"Please do." She shimmied into the first petticoat. "What time is it?" She pulled on the second.

"Almost six," came his voice, through the door. "I hope Mrs. Friar saved some dinner. I could eat a raw moose."

Maggie smiled, then just as suddenly, frowned. No corset, no bustle. The only ones she'd brought were currently draped over a bathroom fixture, still dripping seawater from their whalebone stays and padding. Well, she'd just have to go without, that was all there was to it. She pulled the dress over her head, glancing in the mirror before the first fold of skirt covered her face. Oh, bother! Now she'd have to fix her hair, too. Standing on one's head never did anything positive for one's coif.

"Maggie, I wonder if—"

His words were cut short by a sudden *thud* and a sick, ripping sound. Maggie threw open the bathroom door in time to see Grady, just landing in the center of the room from what must had been a colossal leap.

"Jesus!" he gasped as he touched solid flooring, and stared at the bed.

There, jutting up a good six inches through the center of the mattress, was a wide, shiny blade, still quivering slightly.

SEVENTEEN

"FASCINATING," MAGGIE HEARD GRADY MUTTER UNder his breath. "Ah. Perhaps not."

They were both on the floor, but Maggie was peering beneath the bed, while Grady had crawled all the way under. She heard a little *squeak-squeak-squeak* sound, and glanced up just in time to see the blade retract through the hole it had made in her bed linens. And then burst back through again at the same moment Grady said, "Damn!"

Maggie's hand went to her heart. "Good gravy! If I'd been in the bed, it would have—"

"Sliced through you like warm butter?" quipped Grady, his voice muffled, as the blade retracted again. "At least the end would have been quick. The damn thing nearly buggared me!"

Maggie heard a *click* and then another *click*, and then Grady's feet, then legs, then backside, wiggled out from under the bed. His torso emerged at last. He looked up at her, a clump of dust riding the top of one ear. "Stand back," he said. "I don't trust this thing."

Maggie was already moving to a safe distance. Actually, she was across the room. She thought for just a second that perhaps outside, in the hallway, would have been better.

Grady stood up and brought with him a three-legged contraption. From this base, it rose into a single, thick, cylindrical tube about four inches wide and twelve inches long.

"Thought I was going to have to ruin my penknife," Grady said, sitting down on the bed, "but it wasn't screwed down." He tilted it, and she saw the screw holes, one in the foot of each of the three legs. "It was wedged, actually. I don't believe he counted on the bed being quite so close to the floor."

Maggie sat next to him. "How does it work?"

"Well," said Grady, with just a tinge of superiority—he did love his gadgets, "he would have wedged it under the bedboards. It's on a spring. A rather nasty, heavy spring, if I do say so. See these little marks here?" He pointed to little notches on either side of the cylinder's rim. "They mark the blade's edges. Quite clever, really. He could line it up so that the blade would go between the boards. Not lose any of its impact, so to speak. And then he would have removed the safety."

Gently, Grady eased away a small hook at the bottom. "And then it was armed. So to speak. The tiniest vibration would have set of off. You getting into bed, for instance."

With a forefinger, he tapped the side of the cylinder. Instantaneously, the blade flew from the cylinder—flew all the way across the room to shatter a glass picture frame and embed itself in a print of Washington crossing the Delaware.

Puzzled, Grady peered into the cylinder. "I would have sworn that spring was fastened down . . ."

Maggie was on her feet. "Good gravy! Be careful with that!" She walked to the wall and wrested free the blade. Which, she noted, had neatly decapitated Mr. Washington.

It had started out as a hunting knife, the sort her father had referred to as an Arkansas toothpick—a wicked thing, long and wide and honed on both sides, serrated on one. Not the sleek, clean blades that she liked to throw, but a weapon used by barbarians *on* barbarians, for the sole purpose of killing and maiming each other. The grip (and the part of the blade that it sandwiched) had been sawed through about halfway down—to enable it to fit in the cylinder, she supposed—and a long, thick spring hung down from it.

She stared at this particularly ugly weapon for a time, then turned to Grady. "Come on. Let's go down to dinner."

"You want to eat? Now?"

She nodded. "Yes. And keep quiet about this little surprise. I want whoever set it to think the spring hasn't sprung yet."

Grady got to his feet and handed her the base. "Yes, my liege," he said, shaking his head. Then he looked past her, at the ruined print. "Oh. Sorry, Mr. President."

A few minutes later, Maggie—her hair restored to some semblance of fashion—and Grady made their way into the dining room.

"I do hope we're not too late," Maggie said with a smile.

Mercury, head propped on one hand, looked up and smiled sheepishly. "Nope. It's just grab what you can." He swept an arm over the table, which was laden with cold cuts and salads and some leftovers of questionable origin. "Mrs. Friar took a tray up to Mrs. Kellogg, I think."

Grady pulled out Maggie's chair. He said, "And the others?"

Mercury shrugged. "Carlisle's in the game room. Don't know where Gus is. I've been thinkin' that he looked kind of familiar."

Maggie saw Grady flick his eyes toward her. She calmly helped herself to the roast beef and two slices of bread. "Yes?"

"Well, I placed him," said Mercury, passing her the butter.

Maggie took it. Next to her, Grady was piling ham and cheese on two thick slices of brown bread, seemingly oblivious to everything else.

She said, "And?"

Grady reached for the mustard.

"Well, I'm not sayin' he is or he isn't," Mercury replied. He leaned back in the chair, his fingers threaded behind his neck, his elbows cocked out to the sides like chicken wings. "He's a nice enough fella, and I wouldn't want him to get in trouble. But I'd almost swear on the Good Book that he's got himself a striking resemblance to a boy that took me for near five hundred dollars in a land deal. This was in New Mexico, about fifteen years back. He's skinnier now. Hair's different, and he didn't have the mustache before, but I think it's him."

Grady being finished with the mustard pot, Maggie dipped a knife and spread some on her sandwich. "Are you going to keep me in suspense?" she asked before she put the whole shebang together and raised it to her lips.

"Oh. Sorry." Mercury unclasped his fingers to scratch his head. He smiled. "Bartlett, he was called. Reuben Bartlett."

The bite of roast beef sandwich which Maggie had been in the process of swallowing lodged in her throat. Grady looked up from his ham and cheese just long enough to slap her on the back.

"Thanks," she muttered, after she re-swallowed it.

"Um," said Grady, who was busy chewing again, and already reaching for more bread.

Mercury stared at her with arched brows. "You okay?"

She set the sandwich down and reached for the water pitcher. "Yes, fine. You just caught me a little off guard, that's all." The water poured, she took a long drink. "Reuben Bartlett, eh? You're sure?"

Mercury shook his head. "Well, like I said, I don't think I could swear to it in a court of law. I mean, he sure doesn't *act* the same. Fella I knew was all big city polish . . . Well, what do I know? I'm a hick. But he sure wasn't from the West."

Maggie said, "Then what makes you think he's the same man as this Bartlett?"

Grady, who had put to waste his first sandwich and was currently slathering the second with mustard, said, "Mags, I think he's right."

She turned toward him. "Go on."

"Well, when— Half a second." Grady looked toward the lobby, where Mrs. Friar, an empty tray under her arm, was limping toward them from the bottom of the stair.

"Good evening, Mrs. Friar," Grady said before he took an enormous bite of his sandwich.

"Evenin'." She entered the dining room and would have shuffled right past them, to the kitchen, if Maggie hadn't stopped her.

"How is Mrs. Kellogg doing?" she asked.

The housekeeper stopped. "Well, how do you think she'd be doin'? Lost her husband. Saw him murdered before her eyes, poor lamb. All red-faced and weepy-eyed and soggy from cryin', that's how she is. Ain't had the heart to tell her about Mrs. Perch, yet."

Maggie thought she saw something resembling pity in the woman's ruined face, and suddenly she felt very sorry. Not so much for Temperance Kellogg as for the housekeeper. It must be awful to be born with an unbearable face, awful to lose a husband, more horrible yet to have a stroke and see that unfortunate face become grotesque. Maggie said, "We all feel very deeply for Mrs. Kellogg's loss. Please don't misunderstand."

Mrs. Friar pursed her lips. Well, one side of them. She said, "A body'd never know it, the way you're chowin' down. That's the last of the beef you've got sittin' on that sandwich. And looks like he just polished off the last of the ham."

Mouth full, Grady smiled sheepishly.

Maggie said thoughtfully, "Mrs. Friar, I'm sorry to ask you again, but are you absolutely *certain* there's not another soul on this island?"

The housekeeper rolled her eyes. "Miss Maguire, I get myself up outta bed every morning at five o'clock. I get dressed and go out to the barn, milk six cows and muck their stalls and throw them outside with their feed. I grain and water ten horses, shoo them out into the paddocks with ten flakes of hay, then muck *their* stalls. Then I gather up all the eggs—and some'a them hens is territorial—and feed the chickens, and that just takes us up to six-thirty in the morning. Then I got to come up to the lodge again and wash the muck off and start in on breakfast for you folks. Now, you really think I'd do all that work if there was anybody else here to do it?''

Maggie knew when she was beaten. Before the housekeeper could launch into a further diatribe about how much extra effort a bunch of unexpected guests had cost her, she said, ''Thank you, Mrs. Friar. Was Gus, that is, Mr. Thorpe, upstairs?''

''I didn't go bangin' on all the doors, Miss Maguire. And how come you're askin' the questions? How come it's not Mr. Marchand, here, or Mr. Carlisle?''

''Why not me?'' Grady asked, around a mouthful of sandwich.

Mrs. Friar gave a snort.

''I'm just the curious sort, Mrs. Friar,'' Maggie said. She hardly wanted to confess her profession at the moment, least of all to the housekeeper. ''I'm good at puzzles,'' she added.

The other woman frowned. ''Not so good as to keep that shark from eatin' poor Mrs. Perch. Law, I thought I'd never live to see the like!'' With that, she turned on her heel and disappeared into the kitchen.

''Live to see the like'a what?'' came a new voice. Gus stood in the doorway. Moving forward to pull out a chair, he remarked, as he sat down, ''By jingo, this is sure a spread! You wanna pass down that— Oh. Well, somebody wanna pass down that rat cheese?''

EIGHTEEN

GRADY PASSED THE CHEESE, THEN THE LIVER SAUsage and the pickle loaf, then the tomatoes and the onions and the mustard and the brown bread. And then, while Maggie and Mercury watched Gus in what he could only take to be stunned admiration, Grady pushed back his chair.

He couldn't be of any more help to Maggie at the moment, unless he wanted to pass Gus the jarred apricots or pickled beets. And frankly, ever since she'd told him to "go play with the Edison," he'd been itchy to do just that.

"If you'll excuse me?" he said. Maggie turned her head long enough to shoot him a curious look, but what did she expect him to do? Stay and tell her why Mercury was right about Gus? No, that should wait until they were alone.

Besides, it didn't really have anything to do with the case. So what if Gus was the small time con man Grady had placed just that afternoon, just minutes before Maggie had clubbed him on the back of the head. Maybe he'd bilked Sam Warden out of some money—or tried to. Warden held a grudge, that was for certain. Gus—he couldn't call him Reuben Bartlett—must have cleaned Warden pretty good.

Grady smiled as he entered the game room. A crook Gus Thorpe might be, but Grady had to hand it to him. Fleecing Sam Warden!

Rance Carlisle was slouched down, asleep in one of the leather chairs, and Grady stepped over his legs on his way to the Edison. What an instrument! So shiny and new, with nary a smudge on its brass. At home, his machine was shinier, though. Unless . . .

No, Otto wouldn't touch it. Otto would wait until he got back to San Francisco. Or would he? A picture suddenly popped into his mind of the grizzled old toymaker, Ozzie purring at his side, unscrewing the amplifying trumpet with a gleeful smile.

Anger surged through him, then left him just as quickly—if Otto took his Edison apart, it served him right. After all, it had sat there, untouched, for . . . What was it? Two weeks?

As he began to hunt for another cylinder—something with music, perhaps—to the accompaniment of Carlisle's snores, Grady wondered what in the world he'd ever seen in Muriel Cosgrove. No, Miriam.

See that? he thought. *You've forgotten her name already.*

What had he ever seen in Miriam? Besides the obvious, that was. She certainly had a lot of "obvious." What he needed was a nice, stable, intelligent girl, like Maggie. Why did she have to run around in her underwear half the time? It made a fellow feel . . . uncousinly, if there were such a word.

No, not like Maggie, he chided himself. Always running off and getting herself—and him—into fixes. Bound for danger, and too much of the time, for no pay! Running off to islands where there were murderers running around and bodies falling and sharks and—

"Damn and blast," he said under his breath, and stood up. No more cylinders, not in the cupboards or the shelves. Well, he'd just have to play with the one that was on it. He would have liked to hear something else, that was all. Perhaps Edison's very own voice!

He sat down next to the machine, but paused before he started it to cock an ear to the conversation in the next room. Light and conversational, from what he could hear over Carlisle's snoring. Mrs. Friar was back, clearing the table. Maggie sounded awfully well-behaved, although how she could stand to be, having just nearly missed being skewered by that blade under her bed, was beyond him. He felt like knocking each and every one of the guests in the jaw, just on general principle.

Well, maybe not Temperance Kellogg. But Mrs. Friar was another matter entirely. No more ham? No more roast beef? Gad, what was a fellow to do?

Grady gently turned the crank, and the voice of Sam Warden began, scratchily, to fill the air.

But Grady stopped suddenly. Feeling suddenly as if a cold draft had entered the room, he stood up, walked around Rance Carlisle's legs and went to the door.

He cleared his throat. Maggie looked up, along with Mercury and Gus. Grady said, "Maggie? The recording's been changed."

"Well, would he have had to melt the wax to make a new recording?" Maggie insisted. They had, all but Temperance, moved into the game room, and Mercury had woken Rance. "To recoat the cylinder or something?"

"Maggie, I don't know *everything*," Grady grumbled as he fussed with the machine. "I've never tried to put anything on one."

Maggie glanced out over the room. Mercury, Gus, and Rance sat forward, waiting. Mrs. Friar leaned in the doorway, clutching a dishtowel. "Don't know why I have to listen," she said, although Maggie noticed her fingers were bloodless. "This don't concern me."

"Just a minute," Maggie said, and turned back toward Grady. Actually, she didn't think this was such a wonderful idea, playing the recording for everyone. Well, everyone but Temperance. She would've liked to listen to it once or twice, first.

Oh, well.

"Ready," said Grady.

Maggie nodded.

"Hello again, my friends!" said the tinny voice. "Two down and the rest to go. No, check that. Three down. I have to admit, I hadn't counted on Andrews. Someone was quicker than I thought! Well, a little change of plan keeps one on one's toes, don't you think?

"And it was so nice of Phoebe to take that dip after lunch. She always was a thoughtful girl. Always thinking ahead. She thought ahead when she took twenty thousand dollars and ran out on me. *My* twenty thousand. Back then, she was going by the name of Rose McDonald. Of course, I doubt that was her real name. I doubt she could remember her real name, she'd taken so many phonies.

"Well. After all the marks she'd shaved and throats she'd cut, the shark seemed appropriate, don't you think? Much better than if it had been, say, Carlisle."

Rance turned beet red and began to grope for his pills.

"Tsk, tsk, Rance, old boy," the recording went on. "We could have made a killing on that cattle deal, but no, you had to weasel out on me.

"And then there was good old Kellogg. The axe in his back was fitting, very fitting. Now, I wonder who's going to be next. Sweet dreams, all!" The voice laughed, and then the recording came to the end.

Rance must have taken his pills, for his shade had backed down to a flushed pink. Mrs. Friar was at his side, fanning him lackadaisically with her dishtowel.

Gus swallowed visibly. Mercury stared at the Edison, his mouth open.

Maggie knew it was hopeless to ask who'd had access to the machine. They all had. Any one of them could have found a few minutes to be alone in the room. Any one of them could have made the recording. And the quality was so poor that it could have been anyone's voice, from President Arthur to Queen Victoria. Well, perhaps not Queen Victoria. The accent would have given her away.

Instead, she said to Rance Carlisle, "Is that true? Were you involved in a business venture with Sam Warden?"

Carlisle looked up. His color was normal, now. He waved away Mrs. Friar, and said, "Yes. All right? I'd like to go to my room, if you wouldn't mind."

He started to stand, but Maggie motioned him back down, saying, "I'd like to hear it, Mr. Carlisle. All of it."

Carlisle sighed theatrically. "Well, there's not much," he said. "About eight years ago this Warden fellow approached me, said he had this thing all worked out to swindle some back East boys, and all he needed was some cattle and a man who could talk. Well, I've got the cows, and I sure can talk, and I don't much care for back East boys."

"Except that they eat beef," Grady whispered.

Maggie stepped on his foot. "Go on, Mr. Carlisle."

"Well, that's about it. I backed out at the end. Got to thinking how it might put me out of business for real if I got found out. I worked too hard to build the Circle C to take a flier on some quick money, even if it was near a fortune."

As Grady wrested his toes from beneath Maggie's heel, she said, "And what do you consider a fortune, Mr. Carlisle?"

Rance frowned. "I would'a made about forty thousand outta the deal, if that's what you're asking, Miss Maguire. And I have to say, I still don't understand why you seem to be in charge of this whole shebang. Seems to me we'd be better off if we—"

"That's all, Mr. Carlisle," Maggie said dismissively.

"I won't be hushed, by God! We've got to quit this female shilly-shallyin'! I'm not going to end up like Kellogg. All you people listen to me. We're going to arm ourselves with whatever's handy. Guns, knives. Hell, farm tools! Pitchforks, if that's all you can find. And then we're going to camp out right here in this room until—"

"Mr. Carlisle!" Maggie shouted over him. "We will do no such thing. If we arm ourselves with pitchforks and rakes, we'll be likely to kill each other off by accident, which I'm sure would please Sam Warden immensely.''

Carlisle was on his feet. He turned toward Gus and Mercury. ''Are you going to keep listening to this *woman*?''

Grady stood, too. ''She knows what she's doing, Carlisle,'' he said, rather calmly, Maggie thought. ''She's had some experience.''

''As what?'' the thick man thundered, his face growing red again. ''What is she, a police matron or something? Does she read crime novels? Have her purse snatched once? That makes her an expert?''

''No,'' said Maggie, anger keeping her voice low and more steady than she'd expected. She hadn't wanted to do this, by Carlisle was forcing her hand. ''I am not a fancier of crime novels, Mr. Carlisle. I find them much to far-fetched and melodramatic.'' She reached into her pocket and, producing a small silver case, plucked a card from it and handed it to him.

He stared at the card for a moment, then looked up at her again. ''Bah!'' he spat. Tossing the card to the floor, he stormed from the room, nearly knocking Mrs. Friar down in his haste.

Grady moved next to Maggie and crossed his arms. ''Well. I guess he told you.''

''Charming man,'' Maggie whispered, replacing the card case. ''He might be right about the sleeping in one room part, though.''

''I'd rather be murdered than share a couch with Carlisle for five minutes,'' Grady muttered under his breath.

''A detective?'' said Mercury. He had rescued the card from the floor and was staring at it.

''A detective, eh?'' said Mrs. Friar, as if she had known it all along. ''Reckon that explains a bit.''

''A *private* detective?'' said Gus, who was squinting at the card Mercury held. He looked up, worried. ''Like them stock detectives back home?''

''Nothing like a cattle detective, Gus,'' replied Grady.

"Nothing at all. Those boys are hired killers."

Mercury stuck the card in his pocket. "What kind, then?"

"The kind," said Maggie, wearily, "that sent Sam Warden to prison four years ago."

NINETEEN

"WELL," SAID GRADY, AS HE LET HIMSELF INTO Maggie's room, "I have to hand it to Gus."

"Reuben," said Maggie, distractedly juggling three apples she'd nipped from the table.

"Whatever," continued Grady. "He certainly can keep it up. His act, I mean. All the way down to the cellar he was talking about you, wanting to know 'just what kinds'a cases Miz Maguire is lookin' into.' Like that. And by the way, please, never again ask me to carry a body to the root cellar after it's been dead almost twenty-four hours." He slouched into a chair, pulled out his handkerchief, and dabbed at his nose delicately. "It was . . . repugnant."

Maggie kept on juggling. "Stop exaggerating. It couldn't have been that bad. It's only been sixteen or seventeen hours, at most." She noticed he'd slouched in the chair, taking on his most woebegone posture. She stopped the apples, catching the last two in one hand. "Of course Gus kept it up. He doesn't know he's been found out yet."

Grady looked up. "You believe Mercury, then?"

"And you," she said, smiling faintly. "After all, you're the one with the solid gold memory."

"Yes," he said, assuming a proud, yet humble, rather faraway look. "It is rather impressive, isn't it?"

"Besides, I already knew he wasn't some cowpoke from

New Mexico. Well, I practically knew it. It was just on the tip of my brain.''

Grady cocked a brow. ''Oh?''

''First of all, he can't decide which way to eat. When he's in character—which he is the vast majority of the time—he handles his cutlery like he was born in a barn.'' Maggie started juggling the apples again. ''But every once in a while he'll forget and use the right fork, or cut his meat like a gentleman instead of a hick. Last night, at dinner, he even asked Temperance to pass the grape scissors. Now, how would a cowhand know about grape scissors? He caught it right away, of course, but not before I did. Just subtly, mind you, but it hit a wrong note. No, I had a feeling he wasn't who he said he was,'' she finished, with some satisfaction. Then, seeing the disappointed look on Grady's face, she added, ''But I didn't know *who* he was. How did you?''

Grady straightened slightly. ''While we were carrying Roman Kellogg, he said something—Gus, of course, not Roman—that made me think of the old posters. You know, the ones I file in the back room?''

''Yes?'' said Maggie, thinking of the cartons and cartons and cartons stacked against the wall in what was supposed to have been their communal dining room. He'd been promising to clean them out for years.

''Well, it didn't take long to put a name to the face once I got to thinking about it. I would have had it sooner,'' he added, ''if only there hadn't been so blasted much going on around here.''

''History?'' said Maggie, her attention on the apples.

Grady closed his eyes. ''Reuben Bartlett, alias John Ruby, alias Hank Slocum and others too numerous to mention. Wanted for petty thievery, confidence games, land swindles, things of that like. Nothing so big as bilking Sam Warden. And will you please stop juggling?''

''No,'' Maggie said with a smile. She should have taken a fourth apple while she was at it. She eyed the rubber balls on the bureau top, wondering if she could snag one without stopping. ''I very much doubt Sam would have gone to the police. What did you make of the first part of his little message?' ''

''Which was that?''

''The part about Andrews.'' It had been bothering her.

He thought for a moment. ''Yes. Bizarre, wasn't it? He made it sound like Andrews was killed by accident.''

Maggie nodded. ''The question is, how do you accidentally pick someone's lock, creep up on them in the dark, and stab them in their sleep? I could understand it if was really dark, but there was a moon last night. And we all knew which was Andrews's room.''

''Mistaken identity?'' offered Grady. ''I once asked the wrong girl to the cock fights by accident.''

''Hardly the same, I think.'' Maggie caught the apples and placed them on the bureau. ''I do hope you don't go to those filthy things. Poor chickens.'' She stared at him.

''I wasn't planning that we'd get that far,'' he said. ''I don't go in for that sort of thing. As if you didn't know.''

''Just checking,'' she said, and sat on the edge of the bed. ''Don't worry,'' she said when Grady leapt up. ''I checked. I checked four times, actually.''

He sat down again.

''All right,'' she began. ''Here's what we have so far. Warden is on the island. Warden is one of us. I think we can delete you and me from the list right away.''

''Magnanimous of you,'' Grady said dryly.

''Thank you,'' she said, without missing a beat. ''I think we can count the ladies out, too. Phoebe, of course, since she's—you'll pardon the expression—fish bait, but also Temperance Kellogg and Mrs. Friar.''

''Why?'' asked Grady. ''I rather fancied Mrs. Friar. I mean, for the killer. What a masterful makeup!''

Maggie made a face at him. ''Because she and Temperance and Phoebe witnessed Roman Kellogg's murder, that's why. Unless Mrs. Friar could hurl an axe nearly a hundred yards and then convince Roman to turn and face her, I seriously doubt she's our murderer."

Grady snorted. "Spoilsport."

"Roman Kellogg and Mr. Andrews are out of the running, too, for obvious reasons," she went on, thinking of the root cellar and its contents. "So we're left with Mercury, Gus, and Rance."

Grady stuck out his feet and crossed his arms. "Troublesome. Gus's history doesn't match, Mercury's been too busy running for the last twenty years, and Carlisle can't walk twelve feet without taking a heart pill. I still vote for Mrs. Friar."

Maggie changed the subject. "Everyone all tucked in?"

"Gus and Mercury went straight to their rooms after we came up from the root cellar. Mercury locked his door, and I heard Gus not only lock his, but put a chair under the knob. Temperance and Carlisle had their doors closed. Temperance was still in there. Put my ear to the door, and she's still sniffling. And Carlisle was locked in, too, and pacing. I saw his shadow crossing the light under his door, back and forth."

"Good work," Maggie said. She glanced at the clock, which read nearly ten-thirty. It was time to do some serious thinking. Alone.

"You have that 'you're dismissed' look on your face," Grady said, standing up.

"Oh. Sorry," she said. "Get yourself some sleep, and do check the bed first."

"Are you mad?" he replied, hand on the latch. "I intend to check under each piece of furniture, behind every door, and wad towels in all the cracks."

She laughed. And then, when he had stepped out and was closing the door behind him, she had a thought. "Grady? Have you seen the cat today?"

"Come to think of it, no. Why?"

She went to the door. "No reason. But it does seem odd, doesn't it?"

Grady sighed. "No, Maggie. A six-legged foal is odd. A missing cat is curious."

"I thought all cats were—"

He threw up his hands in mock exasperation. "Oh, go to bed! And for God's sake, lock the door behind me!"

For a long time, Maggie lay awake, staring at the shadowy ceiling, her head on the slight lump created by the Colt pistol under her pillow. Thank goodness she'd packed it out of habit.

Why was Warden surprised by Andrew's death? He certainly hadn't committed suicide. That knife hadn't just materialized in his chest. Was it possible they had two killers instead of one?

After all, she'd figured out that anagram in no time at all.

Maybe somebody else had, too.

She played a game of eeny-meeny-miney-moe with the remaining suspects. It couldn't be Gus, because Gus's past was accounted for. Or was it? Grady wasn't wrong often, but he could be wrong about that Reuben Bartlett business. After all, Mercury had suggested it, and Mercury was, after all, one of his idols. The story Gus had told Grady and which Grady had relayed, about Gus being a poor ranch hand with a good friend that Sam Warden had bilked . . .

Suddenly, it seemed overly melodramatic. All it needed was an orphan on an ice floe. With grape scissors.

And what about Mercury? That story he'd told her, the one about Warden's men attacking him in the middle of a cross-country race—a race that had taken place twenty-five years ago. There was no possible way she could check it. He'd have to know that. They had no proof he was a tailor—well, he did have awfully nice clothes. But they could have been purchased. And, she reminded herself, it was Mercury who had suggested that Gus wasn't who he said he was.

When you suspected that you were suspected (so to

speak), what did you do? Throw some dust in the air, that was what, and Mercury had done just that.

Which—by default, because she got too tangled up in Gus and Mercury to go any further—brought her to Rance Carlisle, the Cattle King. No way to check that ranch of his, no way to be certain it even existed. Oh, he gobbled those pills like they were candy, but maybe they were. Perhaps that vial contained sugar pills, just for their benefit, and he was dashing around the compound, rigging knives and throwing axes willy-nilly.

She even took apart Mrs. Friar, piece by piece. Once again there was no way to check her story, but Captain Harding had recognized her. *Lovely man, the captain*, she thought with a slow smile, then rolled her eyes.

"Business, Magdalena, business," she whispered, and then she thought about Quincy Applegate, waiting patiently back in San Francisco with his actuarial tables . . . No, probably inviting someone else to the theater—the *nerve!*—and dejectedly started over with Gus.

Grady, after checking the bed and the chairs and the doors and the windows, the drawers and the wardrobe; after jamming towels into every opening in the room including the sink drain and bath drain and the rim of the convenience's seat, at last settled gingerly into bed, then remembered that he hadn't locked the door.

"Gad!" he whispered, thumping himself in the forehead, and crept from under the covers to turn the key. He was halfway to the bed again before he did an about-face and jammed a chair under the latch, too. That would keep the bastard out, whoever he was. Or she.

Temperance Kellogg sniffled as she wrote, the pen scratching along the page in her ink stained hand, a wadded hankie in the other.

She had to finish Roman's book. Funny, that she still thought of it as Roman's book. But she had to finish it, had to get the last chapters down before someone thrust an axe into her, too.

The manuscript had taken a turn. A new character had appeared out of nowhere, a person who had walked into a stranger's room and thrust a knife into his chest.

A tear fell on the page, but she scarcely noticed it. She just kept writing, faster and faster.

Gus Thorpe, alias Reuben Bartlett, sat just as he had the night before, smoking a cigarette in the dark. Just enough moonlight peeked through the gaps in the heavy drapes that it enabled him to see his smoke, bluish in the night, and make out (barely) the outlines of the furnishings.

The ready-mades were far superior to those things he rolled during the day, just to keep the farce going, he thought. Well, all right, sometimes they were a little stale, but they weren't lumpy, and it beat all that shifting and licking. Unsanitary.

That Maguire woman was on to him. He'd seen it in a flick of her eyes last night when he'd slipped and asked for the goddamned grape scissors. Grape scissors!

"Shit," he said aloud, and was surprised when he jumped at the sound of his own voice.

Just a flick of the eyes, but that was enough for an old pro like him. Jesus, what a stupid mistake!

He'd hoped that he'd done a good enough job on Grady to convince him with that story about the old man and taking his name and all, and at the time, he was pretty sure he'd been successful. Except that when the Maguire dame produced that goddamned card, he knew he was sunk.

He'd figured her for some kind of private eye, probably amateur, probably the armchair variety, and he'd put a word in that windbag, Carlisle's, ear—very surreptitiously, of course—that if a big cattle baron like himself took over the leadership, they'd sure feel a whole lot more secure. Yesirree Bob, boy howdy.

Well, that backfired, didn't it?

He lit a fresh cigarette off the glowing end of the old one, then stubbed the butt in the ashtray and stared at the new smoke wafting faintly across the room.

Christ. *Now* what?

After a good long pacing session, Rance Carlisle slept with his door locked and his drapes drawn and his little vial of pills on his nightstand.

He also slept with a pistol under the covers, near his right hand.

He turned slightly, and with that, began to snore.

Mercury Marchand, too, was sleeping. Also with his door locked and his drapes pulled. His sleep was not so blissful as Carlisle's though, for he tossed and turned, lashed out with a fist, then turned again.

He woke and found himself in a cold sweat, and in the dim light reached for the pitcher beside his bed.

He poured out a glass of water, and raising it to his lips with shaking hands, whispered, "Jesus." He mopped his brow and took a long drink, draining the glass.

He turned to touch the picture he couldn't see in the gloom, but one he knew was there, one that rested at his side and that brought him comfort. "Good night, Eliza," he whispered, and then he settled back and tried to drift off once more.

He was asleep in five minutes.

Downstairs, Mrs. Friar was the only living person on the island not in bed. She stood on the kitchen stoop, her wrapper pulled tight around her, and called again.

"Kitty, kitty, kitty? Here, Albatross! Here, kitty, kitty, kitty!"

TWENTY

THE NEXT MORNING, MAGGIE WAS JUST BUTTONING her dress when Grady knocked on her door. "Are you all right?" he asked, the moment she let him in.

"Of course," she replied. And then she noticed that while he was dressed, his waistcoat was fastened one button off and there was blood on his left hand. Perspiration beaded his brow, too.

She grabbed for his hand and lifted it, saying, "What happened?" and then, "There's no wound!"

Grady said, "Mind?" and slid into a chair, pulling out his handkerchief and mopping his forehead, then scrubbing at his hand.

"Grady?"

"There is—was—a viper. In my, uh, convenience," he said, eyeing the bloodstained handkerchief which he held at arm's length. "Is the blood poisonous, too?"

"No. There was a s-snake in your toilet?" Maggie felt as if all the blood in her body was draining out through her toes. She also felt the urgent need to sit down, which she did abruptly, on the edge of her bed.

"Yes," said Grady. "Filthy thing." He shuddered, dropped the handkerchief, and clasped himself with both arms. Grady had an almost maniacal fear of snakes, Maggie knew, but to lift the seat and find one staring up from the bowl? That would send anyone into state of the jitters.

Grady was lucky he hadn't had a heart attack!

"What kind is it?" she asked, finally.

"You mean what kind *was* it," he said, a little more calmly.

Oh, wonderful, she thought. *He's flushed it, and who knows where it'll turn up next?* She glanced toward her bathroom door, and imagined it slithering through the pipes, coming closer and closer . . .

But just as she shuddered, Grady said, "I killed it."

"You *killed* it?"

He made a face. "I just said so, didn't I?" He was coming back into his own.

Maggie stood up. "Show me. And fix your vest."

Grady got to his feet sheepishly and nodded toward her bathroom. "First, can I use your, uh . . . ?"

"Of course."

By the time they walked across the hall to Grady's room, and then to his bathroom, he had quite recovered. "If I hadn't jammed towels around the perimeter of the, uh, seat, it could have killed me while I slept."

Maggie bent and gingerly picked up the severed head of the beast—a good sized one, by the looks of it—which was on the floor in front of the carved wood box that enclosed the privy. She stood up and held it toward Grady. "Where's the rest?"

He backed up a step, turning his head away. "Maggie, please. If you wouldn't mind?"

She brought her hand down and deposited the head on the sink's rim. "Sorry." She pointed to the toilet. "Is the rest in here?"

Grady nodded. "My overriding instinct was to flush the blasted thing at least a half-dozen times. I hope you realize—"

"—how you've suffered for me?" Maggie broke in. "Yes, dearest, I fully appreciate it."

Carefully, in case the snake had been traveling with a friend, she lifted the lid and peered in. The snake was alone, though its headless body was still twitching in the bloody water. She recognized the markings immediately.

"A water moccasin? Here?" she said softly.

"Water moccasin? It was a water moccasin?" Grady gripped the sink, then seemed to remember the snake head was there and backed up a step to the doorway.

"Hm," said Maggie, still studying the corpse in the bowl. "I don't know that much about snakes, but I doubt they're indigenous to this region."

"Fine," muttered Grady. "I was very nearly savagely attacked in my most private parts by an *imported* snake. That makes me feel so much better."

Maggie didn't look up. "He must have brought it with him. In fact, I'm certain that brochure said there weren't *any* snakes on this island."

"What brochure?"

"The one in the lobby. Do you have anything to fish this out of here with? And how on earth did you manage to decapitate it?"

"With my razor," he said, still hanging on to the door frame, but standing a little straighter, she thought. "It struck, but I was already slamming down the lid. I just happened to catch the head between the lid and the seat, and, well, my razor was the only thing I could reach." He sighed. "Now I suppose I'll have to get a new one."

"Nothing a little water won't take care of." She glanced up toward the ceiling, at the water tank. "He came from there, you know." She pointed. "Your snake. Warden must have snuck in, stood on the lid, and put him in the tank. When you pulled the chain last night to flush it, you released the little beastie. And he was waiting for you this morning."

"How do you know he didn't come *up* the pipes?"

Maggie shrugged. "Too much of a climb, I think. Plus, I doubt Warden would have taken the chance. It could have ended up in anybody's privy, even his." Gracefully, she gathered her skirts and stepped—half-leapt, really—up atop the seat.

"Oh, God," moaned Grady, who made a motion to help but just as quickly stepped back. "You're not just going to *open* it, are you?"

"No," she said, holding her hand down. "Give me a mirror."

Maggie reached overhead and carefully pushed back the water tank's lid. She angled the mirror above it. Nothing. She pushed it up and all the way back. "Nothing," she reported. "Nothing except . . ." She handed down the mirror and stood on her tip-toes, then reached into the tank, feeling along the back.

"There!" she said, feeling cocky as she replaced the tank's lid and jumped down to the floor. In her hand, she held a bit of wire screen, and the clips that had held it in place. She gave them to Grady. "You see? He put that on the intake from the big tank, up on the roof, so that your little friend couldn't possibly go anywhere except where he ended up."

Hopefully, Grady looked over his glasses. "So this won't happen again?"

Maggie held back her smile. "No. Not unless he's got another snake up his sleeve. Which I doubt," she added hurriedly when she saw Grady's expression, "because our Sam Warden is not one to repeat himself. Both of us were supposed to die, Grady," she went on, thinking of that horrible knife-launching contraption, which currently resided on the bottom shelf of her wardrobe. "Me last night and you this morning. I think, after we're finished here, we'll just go down to breakfast and pretend nothing has happened. It'll be interesting to see if we get a reaction when two corpses show up, asking for eggs."

Grady studied on this for a moment, then nodded. "Will a shoe tree do?" he asked. "To fish it out with, I mean." His head tipped toward the bowl and its cargo, which had finally stopped twitching.

"That," said Maggie, "would be splendid."

• • •

Maggie checked her watch pin as they crossed the lobby, headed toward the dining room. That business with the snake had taken far too long, and it was nearly ten. They'd be lucky if Mrs. Friar hadn't already cleared the table.

As it was, they caught her in the act of picking up plates.

"Well, it's about time!" she huffed, and put a platter, with its few strips of cold bacon, back on the table. "Don't be expecting me to cook for you. You come down late, it's just leftovers."

"Do you treat all your guests this courteously?" asked Grady, who seemed to have forgotten all about the snake, and was already tucking his napkin into his collar with one hand and reaching for a rack of cold toast with the other. You could count on Grady having an appetite, come hell or high water.

"Mrs. Friar, where are the others?" asked Maggie. Aside from the three of them, the room was empty.

The housekeeper was glaring at Grady. Oblivious to all else, he studiously slapped another spoonful of apricot preserves on his toast.

"Mrs. Friar?"

She turned back toward Maggie. "Mrs. Kellogg's still in her room. Took her breakfast up. The others are long gone. And yes," she added, rather nastily, to Grady, "I treat my guests this way when they ain't guests at all, but some sort of murder party that shows up outta nowhere and then starts killing itself off and probably my poor kitty, too, and I've gotta take care of the barns and the livestock and the laundry and the cooking and them all by myself and—"

"The cat hasn't shown its face yet?" Maggie broke in.

The working side of Mrs. Friar's lips began to tremble. "No. No, he hasn't. If something's happened to my little Albatross, I'll . . . I'll . . ."

Suddenly, Mrs. Friar was in Maggie's arms and Maggie was comforting her the best she could, and Mrs. Friar, between sobs, was saying, "He never stays away! Five years now, and he always come in every night, always comes to bed!''

Over Mrs. Friar's quaking shoulder, Maggie saw Grady mouth, *''Albatross?''*

''There, there,'' said Maggie. Rather ineffectually, it seemed, because Mrs. Friar just cried harder. ''When we've got some food in our stomachs, we'll have a look round. All right?''

The housekeeper let go—finally—and stepped back. She grabbed a napkin off the table, gave her nose a honk, and said, ''You'd do that? For me?''

''Of course!'' said Maggie, surprised by the woman's incredulous look. Had no one ever done her a kindness before? ''We have a kitty at home,'' she explained. ''If he went missing, I'd be out of my mind with worry, too.''

Mrs. Friar wiped at her eyes and stood up a little straighter, the familiar frown returning. ''Well, I'm not out of my mind, exactly. It's just that I'm—''

Suddenly, a rifle's report cut the morning's stillness, and from instinct, Maggie hit the floor immediately, taking Mrs. Friar with her.

''What the hell was that!'' shouted Grady, who had dived under the table at the same second, toast in hand, and was staring at her from beneath the tablecloth.

''It's Mr. Carlisle, and let go of me!'' said the housekeeper, shaking her arm free of Maggie's grip. Hand on a chair seat, she levered herself up and stared down at the two of them. ''I unlocked the gun rack for him. Said he was going to shoot that terrible shark.''

Grady crawled to the window and peered over the sill. ''It's Carlisle, all right.''

Another shot sounded and Maggie jumped, in spite of herself.

''And he's shooting at the shark,'' Grady continued. ''I guess. Into the water, anyway. All clear.'' He stood up and came back to the table, and immediately began smearing jam on another piece of toast.

Maggie climbed to her feet. Two more shots sounded, in rapid succession, which didn't seem to faze Grady one bit.

"Suds," she grumbled, under her breath. Louder, she said, "Why is it that you can *always* eat?"

He shrugged, reaching for the bacon. "Might as well die with a full stomach." He looked up, holding the bacon platter toward her. "You want this?"

TWENTY-ONE

A FEW MINUTES LATER, GRADY (ARMED WITH A BACON sandwich) and Maggie (who had snagged the very last piece of cold toast out from under his nose) walked down the front steps of the Wapiti Lodge. Rance Carlisle, having by that time shot off enough rounds that he was having to reload, stood on the beach, his back toward them.

"I think," said Grady, around a mouthful of bread and greasy bacon, "I'm going to have to agree with you. Mrs. Friar is no longer on my list."

"Big of you," said Maggie, wiping her hands on her skirts. "Why?"

Grady swallowed. "She wasn't the tiniest bit surprised to see us." He took another bite, and eyed the empty tennis court longingly. "Wish I could have had a game," he said, chewing distractedly.

They were halfway down the slope by that time. Maggie put her hand in her pocket, gripped the Colt she carried there, and cocked it. With her other hand, she waved. "Mr. Carlisle? Mr. Carlisle!"

He turned and acknowledged the wave, shouting to Grady, "You want to make yourself useful, Maguire, bring a rifle!" and settled another cartridge into the chamber.

"Well, looks like he's out of the running, too," whispered Grady, brushing a few last errant crumbs off his suit.

"Humph," said Maggie, and closed the distance to Carlisle. "Any luck?" she asked him.

He sighted down the barrel for a moment, then let the rifle swing to his side. "Thought I nicked his fin. That one on top that sticks up."

"Dorsal," said Grady, craning his head toward the woods.

"Whatever," replied Carlisle with a frown. "The bastard—pardon me all to hell, Miss Maguire. Can you say bastard in front of a female detective?"

Maggie stared at him.

"I guess you can," he continued, smugly. "The bastard won't surface and a slug doesn't travel far through the water. What sort of crimes do you detect, anyway? Missing knitting needles? Stolen washboards? Deceased lapdogs?"

Maggie crossed her arms. "I don't like your tone, Mr. Carlisle."

"And I don't like yours, missy. Yesterday, when you came into my room to wake me up, I got to thinkin' that maybe we could have us a little arrangement, you know? You're pretty enough. Got a shape on you. But now I'm thinkin' that you're just too damn pushy to be female all the way through, if you happen to get my meaning."

Before Maggie could reply, Grady stepped between them, growling, "Watch your language, Carlisle."

But Carlisle was on a roll. "Are you *really* her cousin?" he asked, in the smarmiest possible tone.

And before Maggie could stop him, Grady hit Rance Carlisle square in the jaw.

It had absolutely no effect.

Carlisle rubbed his face angrily. "You little pipsqueak!" he roared, just before he dropped the rifle and grabbed Grady—who was at an eighty pound disadvantage, at the very least—around the throat.

"Good gravy," Maggie muttered, and gave Carlisle a kick to the back of the knees as, with the heel of her hand, she neatly clipped him just below his ear.

He went down slowly, in stages, and when he finally dropped to his knees he still had a stranglehold on poor Grady's neck. Maggie pried Carlisle's fingers loose, exposing the red prints of his thumbs on Grady's windpipe, and as Carlisle slumped to the sand, Grady whispered hoarsely, "Totally unnecessary, Mags. I would have had him in a minute."

"Of course you would," said Maggie, stooping to feel for Carlisle's pulse. Still strong. Good. She stood and brushed the sand from her skirts, then picked up his rifle and broke it open, fishing out the cartridges. Putting it back down again, and casting the cartridges out over the sand, she said, "That ought to calm him down. Now, to find Mercury and Gus." She began to head for the walking path, back into the trees.

Grady, rubbing his neck while keeping pace with her. "Really, Maggie," he whispered, still throaty and hoarse. "Just one more second, and I would have had him."

After following the wide path through the woods for roughly a half mile, they came to a fork in the trail. Maggie, increasingly aware that they made a very plain target, said, "Which way?"

"Over there's the Majestic View Trail," said Grady, pointing to the left. His voice had recovered from its former hoarseness, although there were still faint red marks on his throat. "The Tropical Isle Trail's the other one."

He swatted a bug on his neck and then, looking at his hand in disgust, reached for his handkerchief. "If you want my opinion, I think we should wait back at the lodge. If Gus or Mercury have already run into Sam Warden, we can't be of any help to them now."

"We could find the body," said Maggie, annoyed because she almost agreed with him. It was almost noon, it was hot, and she was sweating and hungry. One piece of toast did not a breakfast make. And she didn't care for being a sitting duck, so to speak. It grieved her, but she was fairly certain that Mercury had already met his doom and that he was somewhere, out there. She'd already decided Gus was the killer. Well, not exactly *decided*—she couldn't say anything with absolute certainty—but, well, she liked Mercury better. Totally illogical, but how could she be logical about it when she had not one clue to go on? If only she could sit down and think it through!

"Yes, we could find a body," Grady continued, wiping at his hand. "Or we could *be* the bodies." He seemed to search for a clean spot on his handkerchief, then took off his spectacles and began to polish them.

"Did you hear that?" said Maggie, distracted by a small, out of place sound.

"What?" Grady put his glasses back on.

"Shh," hissed Maggie, listening hard.

It came again, very weak and distant.

Grady looked at her. "The cat?"

"Careful," said Maggie, as he stepped off the path and started toward the sound. "It could be a trap, you know."

He was already heading back into the woods, and she followed him, staying in his footprints as much as possible. "For God's sake!" she said. "Don't go so fast! And pick up a stick, feel the footing ahead of you!" She took her own advice, and bent to grab a fallen branch.

Grady stopped, gave a theatrical sigh, and listened again. The plaintive mewing was closer, pathetic and helpless. Maggie pointed to the left and said, "Over there." Grady started ahead until Maggie said, "Stick?"

"What on earth for?"

She sighed. "Because the ground is deep in needles. Because Warden never does the same thing twice. Because he could have been out here digging tiger traps or planting trip wires or anything else you can think of. Big holes filled with spikes. Falling nets that—"

"All right, all right!" Grady cut in, and grudgingly picked up a suitable limb.

They changed course then, each pushing and poking the

dead leaves and fallen needles in their path, Grady slightly ahead and to her left.

"This is ridiculous," Grady muttered. "We're not going to find anything, and in the meantime that poor little cat is—" He jumped back, straight into Maggie, and they both fell in a tangle.

Maggie craned her head past Grady's hip and looked up. His stick was suspended twelve feet above the ground on a rope which dangled from a lithe pine branch.

She hit him on the shoulder. "You were saying?" she scowled. "And get off of me."

Grady crawled off and climbed to his feet, staring up at his stick, muttering, "Well, I'll be a ring-tailed monkey."

"Grady?"

"What? Oh." He held a hand down to Maggie, who took it and scrambled to her feet.

The cat was still mewing sporadically, and the sound was very close. Grady bent to find another stick, but Maggie said, "Wait a minute." She searched the trees to the left, to the right, straight ahead, and then pointed.

"There," she said. "Look up. Oh, the poor thing!" There, about forty feet ahead and a good fifteen feet above the ground, dangled the cat. It had been caught, she thought, around both back legs, just above the hocks. As she watched, Grady staring alongside her, the cat made a feeble attempt to curl its body upward, to get a grip on the rope which had snared it. But it was too weak and it failed, falling back with a small jolt that shook the narrow branch to which the rope was affixed. It mewed again pathetically.

"I wonder who this was for," Grady said under his breath.

"Doesn't matter now, does it?" said Maggie, finding her stick and starting toward the cat, poking systematically through the detritus on the forest floor. "Hang on, kitty. We're coming."

The cat looked straight at her and mewed again, then stopped to try and wash its shoulder.

"Another one," cried Grady. There was a *whoosh* and she turned just in time to see Grady's new stick fly high into the air on the end of another snare, and then catch in the branches. "And that was my best one, too," he grouched, searching the ground for a new limb.

Maggie worked her way under the cat and past it to the trunk of the tree that held it prisoner. A ponderosa pine. Lovely. She'd never be able to climb it in this rig. Sighing, she began to unbutton her dress.

Grady, who was beneath the cat by this time, looked at her and blinked. "What in God's name are you doing!"

She made a face, and slithered out of her dress. "Well, I can't climb a tree in these," she said, pointing toward her skirts. "And you can't do it. No offense." She began to work at the waistband of her petticoats.

Grady, plainly embarrassed not at the insinuation that he wasn't worthy to climb the tree, but at the idea of her stripping to her underwear in broad daylight, said, "What if somebody comes along?" He craned his head this way and that, searching the trees.

One petticoat off. "They'll probably be snared." She smiled. "They'll be too busy dangling to notice me." The second petticoat slid down her legs.

"You could stand on my shoulders?" Grady offered.

She dropped the final petticoat, and stepped from the pile in her pantalets and chemise, thankful that she'd left the corset hanging from her towel rack back at the lodge.

"Give me your knife," she said, and when he grudgingly complied, she stuck it between her teeth and gave a small leap off the ground. She caught the first branch and pulled herself up.

"Grady," she said around the knife as she worked her way up to the next branch, "I could stand on your shoulders all day and *still* not reach it. It's at least fifteen feet, maybe sixteen."

"Gad," he said in disgust. Through the branches, she saw him sit down, and she grinned, despite the needles poking at her and the bark scrapes on her arms.

Higher and higher she went, until she at last reached the branch from which the cat was suspended. It had stopped mewing. She hoped it was silent because it was watching her, not because it was, well, dead. The poor thing had been strung up there all night, after all.

She eased her way out onto the branch, and immediately it started to give. "Grady?" she called.

"Yes, O Naked One, O Dweller in the Tree Tops, O She Who—"

"Grady, just get up and get out here under the cat?"

She heard him grumbling, but he appeared below her. "Mags?" he called. "That branch doesn't look safe."

Ignoring him, she inched out a little farther. The cat's rope was still a good seven feet from her fingertips. "It's all right, kitty. Good Albatross, nice kitty," she said softly, then louder, "I don't know how much this thing is going to bend. Just be prepared to catch the cat, all right?" And then, as she crept forward and felt the limb give even more, she mumbled, "And maybe me, too."

The bough dipped with each forward movement, down, down, lower and lower, its needles shivering, until Maggie could just reach the rope and Grady called out, "Maggie? It's going to break!"

"No it isn't," she shouted back, although she heard a faint cracking sound. "Warden had to climb out here to set it, didn't he?" The rope in one hand, she opened Grady's penknife with the aid of her teeth, wrapped her legs around the branch as tight as she could manage, and began to saw.

Grady was shaking his head. "He could've just stood on the ground. Be careful!"

She was halfway through the rope. It was a thin line—a cotton clothesline, she thought—but that knife of Grady's wasn't so big, either. She would have just thrown it from the ground, except that it had no balance whatsoever. She'd likely end up killing the cat, which had moved a little when she started sawing, but hadn't moved since.

"No one," she replied, "could toss a line up here, especially not one this light. Get ready!"

She cut through the last fibers, and the cat dropped neatly into Grady's waiting arms. She waited, watching, and when he looked up and said, "Alive!" she wanted to cheer. Well, perhaps she'd better wait until she was back on terra firma.

"He could if he'd tied a rock to the end," Grady called, removing the rope from the cat's back legs.

"What?" She couldn't decide. Was it better to back up and then back down the tree, and thcn jump? Or better to just jump to the ground? Her weight had brought the limb down a few feet. If she shifted her weight forward, it might just— The branch made a soft cracking sound again.

"I said, he could have stood on the ground and thrown it if he tied a rock to the end first," Grady said, louder this time.

"Catch!" said Maggie, dropping the knife and the taking a firm grip on the branch. Best to just jump.

Grady, the cat under his arm, bent to pick up his penknife. "Next time, fold it first, will you?" he said, slightly annoyed. "And get down out of that tree and put some clothes on!"

She let her weight roll her off the branch, so that she was hanging by her arms and her weight made it sag even more, and then she dropped. She landed in a crouch but on her feet, and as the branch lashed upward again, said, "See? It's perfectly safe."

There was a loud *crack*, and she jumped back just as the branch broke three feet back from her former handhold and crashed to the ground.

Grady sheltered the cat's eyes. "Don't look," he said, just as Maggie took another step backward, and, with a shriek, was abruptly yanked head over heels. Suddenly, everything was upside down.

As she dangled by one leg, her head four feet above the ground, Grady studied her. At last, he clucked his tongue and said, "Mags. Shame on you. Where was your stick?"

"Shut up," she growled, bobbing up and down and pushing hair out of her eyes. He came closer, until she could see only the middle of his chest, and Albatross, who clung to him, blinking. "Just shut up and give me the knife."

TWENTY-TWO

WITH A SMALL FLOURISH, TEMPERANCE KELLOGG wrote "The End" on the final page of the manuscript, and blotted it.

At last, she thought, the contract was finished and there would never be another one. She was done with horse operas forever. Done with writing of any kind. Roman had put enough money by—enough of *her* money, she thought as she carefully wiped the pen and laid it beside the inkwell—that she could live quite happily doing nothing. Well, almost happily, so long as she could afford her medicine.

The thought reminded her she was feeling a little itchy, a little too in touch with reality, and that was something she fervently wished to avoid. She went into the bathroom—a really grand idea, bathrooms, she must have one added to the house in Seattle. She could do without Roman's study, now. Yes, that would do fine. It even had a fireplace.

Opening the medicine cabinet, she looked from shelf to shelf, frowning, until she remembered where she'd put it. Her hands went down, to the back of the vanity, and latched on to a small bottle. She opened it, took two sips, made a face, then replaced it.

You'd think, she mused as she closed the yawning medicine cabinet and made her way back to the bedroom, *that somebody would do something about the taste.*

She was already feeling better. The laudanum was slowly filtering into her system, yes, but she also felt relieved. "Roamin' Rex" Roman had penned his last book. Mesa Mike had ridden into one last sunset, victorious. Salty Bob had been vanquished one last time. And then, there was her little confession.

Well, confession was good for the soul, wasn't it, even if it had to be through a fictional character.

She realized she'd been standing there, staring at the desk, for nearly ten minutes, thinking the same sentence over and over again. She gave her head a shake that even she realized was wobbly, and pulled out the chair, sitting down not at all like a lady.

First, she slid the discarded pages off the spindle, neatly folded them, and placed them in the wastebasket. An old habit, that. She couldn't stand clutter, no matter how strongly her medicine had kicked in. Couldn't even stand wadded papers in the wastebasket. Even that last time, when she had fallen into the unfortunate habit of taking so much medicine that she couldn't walk, she had yelled at Roman to pick up his goddamn clothes.

She grinned, sloppily. The look on his face! That little impertinence had only earned her another beating, but she'd been too, well, *medicated* to feel it much that day, or even the next. Well, she wouldn't fall into that trap again. Just take it four times a day. Well, sometimes five. And only two sips at a time. Or three.

She remembered where she was again, and placed her hand on the final page with intention of moving it to the bottom of the stack, when there was a soft rap on the door.

Immediately, she felt as if her heart were rising into her throat. The knock came again. She gripped the desk like a life raft.

"W-who is it?" She forced her mouth to work. "Mrs. Friar?" That was it, of course! She'd gotten involved in writing and it was lunchtime already.

But then, through the door, a voice said, "No. I think you know who it is, my little wren."

At once, her knees felt as if they had turned to aspic. Only one man had ever called her that. And he had called her that a very long time ago.

Wobbling, she got to her feet. "Sam?" she said, so faintly that she had to say it again in order for him to hear it.

"Let me in, Wren," came the reply. "Let me in, flutter-bird." So soft. So gentle.

Perhaps he'd forgiven her for what she'd done, all those years ago in Dodge City. Perhaps a man could forgive the woman who turned him in and then skipped town on the first train. After all, she'd been just a girl, just a frightened girl of twenty-one, terrified by the monster she'd seen him turn into.

She'd never seen anyone killed before, let alone by a man she'd thought she loved.

She had, on the whole, been extremely unfortunate in her choices of men. Of course, so had Phoebe, at least in the beginning. They'd smelled Sam on each other the moment they met. Well, perhaps not the precise moment, but eventually. Sam left his mark on a woman like a dog marks a tree, except it wasn't a scent any rain could ever clean away.

The stench of death, that's what it was.

But he wasn't talking like a murderer. At least, not like someone who was going to kill her. "Sam?" she asked once again.

"Open the door, dearest," came the reply. Not like any of the men at the lodge. Like her old Sam, before he started . . . before she realized . . .

Suddenly, she didn't care if he planned to kill her. The laudanum had taken her all the way into its gentle fist, and through its filter Sam's voice seemed inextricably enticing, unalterably welcoming and safe, and filled with love. Just to see him again, just to hold him after twenty years would be enough. Yes, it would be enough after so long with Roman's big, bony fists and his insults. It would be enough after years of writing Roman's books, watching him take the bows, and having no one to love her, not even a little bit.

Sam Warden had loved her once, she was certain. And now she was convinced that he'd loved her all these years, that he still wanted her, needed her.

Taking a deep breath and weaving slightly, she slowly crossed to the door, and she was thinking that perhaps love and death were somehow inextricably intertwined. She had loved Sam, and she had turned him over to the law. She had loved him, and she'd tried to kill him. It seemed only fair that, loving her, he should have the right to decide her fate.

Besides, she just had to see which one of the guests he was.

"Yes, Sam," she said. "I'm coming." And smiling, she unlocked the door.

"Are you still rubbing his hind legs?" Maggie was saying. She and Grady were standing back on the path again, having just come out of the woods, and she was attempting to do something with her hair. Without much success, she was afraid.

"I would if I could reach them," said Grady. Out of the corner of her eye, she caught him peering down at the purring cat, who had burrowed inside his jacket and was peeking out, slit-eyed.

Maggie pulled back another errant wisp, pinned it, and said, "All right. Let's go back to the lodge. I think you made a friend, there."

"He's just grateful," said Grady, obviously smitten. They started walking back.

She caught another loop of hair, which she repinned, and said, "Grady, I've been thinking."

"It's all that blood to the brain," Grady remarked. "Don't worry, it'll go away."

Maggie made a face, which was lost on him since his attention was on the cat. She said, "That Edison. You had a hard time getting yours, didn't you?"

"Pulled strings from here to Christmas and emptied my bank account. Why?"

She reached down and to the side, pulled free a blade of grass, popped one end in her mouth and began to chew. "And the one in the game room here. It was new?"

"Brand spanking, as far as I could tell." He looked at her and scowled. "Why? And spit out that grass. Bound to be filthy."

"Just thinking aloud," said Maggie, who continued to chew thoughtfully, mincing the blade between her front teeth. "Humor me, all right? Mrs. Friar wasn't surprised to see us, was she?"

"No. Did you expect her to be?"

"And Carlisle," she continued, ignoring him. "He wasn't surprised either."

"He was certainly belligerent enough," grumbled Grady, who remembered to feel his throat again.

She glanced over. The red marks were gone except for a faint pink trace where one thumb had burrowed especially deep. She said, "And Mrs. Friar took Mrs. Kellogg her breakfast. So only Gus and Mercury are unaccounted for, right?"

Grady dropped his hand to the cat's head, which had just poked out of his jacket again. "Yes. But you're just going over turf we've already turned."

"Wait," Maggie said, a bit too crossly. She knew she was recovering ground, but she was stuck in a loop she was trying to shake herself out of. "No one has an alibi for Andrews's murder. But all the women are in the clear for Mr. Kellogg's death. And you, of course."

"Golly, thanks," mumbled Grady. He was scratching Albatross's head.

"In the case of Phoebe and the shark," she continued, giving an involuntary shudder, "anyone could have put that shark in the cove, or paid to have it put there. Same thing with the knife under my bed, and the snake in your water closet. The snares could have been placed anytime. Well, provided no one went off the trail to trigger them. Which they wouldn't have done, normally, unless they heard Albatross, here"—she paused to reach over and give the cat a scratch under the chin—"crying for help."

"So basically," Grady said, "you're saying that you don't know squat."

"Don't be vulgar," said Maggie, with a resigned sigh. "And yes, you're right. I suppose I am at sea, Mr. Andrews's death notwithstanding. I still think there's something funny about that one."

Grady, who seemed to be lost in thought, walked on in silence.

She walked for a while beside him, and then kicked at a stone in her path. "I'm just feeling so blasted helpless! I mean, good gravy! I've managed to cut down the list of suspects to the surviving men! Some detective I am. I have this horrible feeling that I'm not going to solve it until there's only one left, and then what kind of reputation will follow me around? Presuming I'm still alive, of course. Three people are dead already, with five to go."

"Mags?" Grady, who obviously hadn't been listening to a word she said, stopped suddenly. "Carlisle didn't take a pill."

She stopped, too. "What?"

"When he choked me," Grady said. "I mean afterward. He was angry, and choking a man certainly requires some physical exertion. And he didn't take one of his famous heart pills."

"Of course not!" Maggie said, and rolled her eyes. "I clipped him. He was out cold."

"Mags, he wasn't even red in the face."

Maggie worked her jaw back and forth, biting off the

grass between her teeth, then spitting it out. "Good point," she said, casting aside the remainder, and started walking again.

Of course, it didn't really prove anything. She could have knocked Carlisle silly before he started the palpitations, or whatever it was he had. He'd never said. And as much as she wanted to believe Carlisle was their man, she just couldn't. He was too outwardly nasty for someone who had plotted to murder them all, too obvious. Too . . . well, larger than life.

The path opened to the lawns, then, and the lodge, impressive as always, popped into view. Carlisle was no longer on the beach. No one was outside.

"No," she said, puffing an annoying wisp of hair off her face. "It's not Carlisle. He just doesn't fit the pattern. Too hostile, I think. After all, if you were a murderer, would you take on a demeanor that called attention to yourself? All his bragging about the Circle C and his blasted cows. Does that sound like the same sort of temperament that would put a snake in a man's privy? Would he make a pass at the woman investigating him? Would he try to throttle another investigator in broad daylight?"

Grady screwed up his face and said, "Don't remind me." And then he hoisted his brows. "When did he make a pass at you?"

She waved a hand dismissively. And off the top of her head, she said, "I think I know who our murderer is."

"Well? The suspense is killing me."

"As much as I'd like to believe it's Rance Carlisle, I can't. And I honestly don't think it's Mercury, either. That leaves—"

"Gus?" Grady broke in. "Our little Gus, who took the last name of his dear and dying old friend?" He hiked his brows. "On the other hand, our little Gus, who's gone by a dozen names and bilked who knows how many people . . . But, Gus? Killing people?"

"How do you know Gus *isn't* Sam Warden?" she insisted, as much to convince herself as Grady. "Certainly, he's full of that cowboy slang, but we already know that's just a front. Besides, there's that thing about the grape scissors, and he takes his hat off all the time! He never wears it in the lodge."

Grady hiked his brows. "Huh?"

Maggie sighed, and reached for another handful of hair that had gone trailing down her back. "A real cowboy only takes his hat off when he goes to bed. And even then, it's the last thing."

Smiling, Grady chucked the cat under its chin. "And how, pray tell, do you know that?"

"I once interviewed some—" She felt heat race up her cheeks, and snapped, "Very funny. Come up with some dates and figures, Grady. Prove me wrong. If you can document that Gus and Sam were in different places on the same date—any date—then you win."

She gave up on her hair. She'd just have to walk into the lodge looking like the wreck of the Hesperus, that was all.

Grady kept walking. "Now, you know, Mags, that I can't prove any such thing, not without getting off the island," he said, evenly, in that calm, no nonsense voice he always used when he thought she was making a mistake. Lord, but it was annoying!

In what she hoped was a persuasive tone, she said, "Well, we can't get off the island until tomorrow, and it's highly likely that at this rate, we'll all be dead by then. Grady, it has to be either Gus or Mercury."

"*Probably* has to be," he muttered. And then louder, he said, "I just can't see Gus hanging little Albatross, here, up a tree."

"Can you see Mercury doing it?"

"Well, no."

"Had you ever seen Mercury before Sunday?" she asked, hoping he'd say yes, he certainly had.

But he said, "No," and kept walking up the lawn.

"Maggie, you're talking through your hat. Tell the truth. You haven't the faintest notion, have you? Be truthful."

He was right, of course. She'd just hoped he'd point out something she'd missed, some detail that would lift the veil from her eyes. But no, all he had was common sense.

Suddenly, a wave of shivers ran through her. Why hadn't she thought of it before! She stopped suddenly, and he walked on three paces before he seemed to realize she wasn't with him and turned to face her.

"Grady?" she said, trying to hold back her excitement, but having little success. "Earlobes," she half-shouted. "A man can disguise a lot of things about himself. He can make his nose bigger or longer or wear wigs or dye his hair or put lifts in his shoes or slump, but there's one thing he can't change."

"His earlobes," said Grady, who remained annoyingly blas. "So?"

"But Grady, you've seen pictures of him. Old ones, granted, but pictures! Surely you can remember—"

He shook his head, and her heart sank. "Maggie, those pictures were so old and of such poor quality . . . There were only two of them, anyway. I'm sorry, but even if I had them in front of me now, I wouldn't be able to tell you whether or not the man had ears, let alone describe the lobes to you."

They began to walk again, and Maggie was silent, lost in a turmoil of thought. Gus or Mercury, Mercury or Gus. Or Carlisle.

Papa? she thought, glancing heavenward. *What would you do?*

And she imagined she heard the General's voice, answering right back, *Why, pack up and move the carnival to the next town, Magdalena, m'girl!*

"Thanks a lot, Papa," she muttered.

"What?" said Grady, opening the door for her. She hadn't realized it, but they'd come all the way up the slope and climbed the steps to the lodge.

"Nothing," she said, and stepped inside. She could hear Mercury's voice coming from the dining room, then Carlisle's voice over it, demanding something or other.

"Well, at least *someone's* still alive," said Grady, far too chipper for her taste. "Personally, I think we should have taken Carlisle's advice. You know, armed ourselves and locked the whole crew in one room?"

Maggie cocked her head back so she could look down her nose at him. "These people couldn't spend fifteen minutes together in a locked room, let alone a day or two. You can't even keep them at the lodge! They're out running or shooting at sharks or swimming or taking nature hikes through the woods! Mrs. Kellogg's the only one with any sense, if you ask me," she finished. "I might just go lock myself in my room, too."

Grady smiled softly. "Sure," he said. "And I'm going to marry Queen Victoria."

Maggie sighed. "You go ahead into lunch," she said, heading for the staircase. "I'm going to do something with my hair, first. Oh, I do hope Gus isn't dead."

"You might want to fix your petticoats, too," said Grady, easing Albatross out of his jacket. The cat clung to him, kneading.

"What?" Maggie looked down at her skirts, then around to the back. One petticoat was dragging three inches below her hemline and was coated with grime. "Since the trees?" she asked with a sigh.

Grady grinned, and wordlessly started toward the dining room.

A few moments later, when Maggie was upstairs and halfway down the hall and considering whether she should tap on Mrs. Kellogg's door, just to check on her, she heard Mrs. Friar's delighted shriek of "Albatross!"

Well, at least someone was happy.

TWENTY-THREE

"ANYBODY SEEN GUS?" GRADY ASKED, HELPING himself to the mashed potatoes. Mrs. Friar had set a decent—if eclectic—table: cold roast venison, potatoes, hot sausages and sausage gravy, green beans, pickled onions, thick-sliced sourdough bread, and a cold cucumber salad. He ladled gravy over his potatoes and considered the salad.

"What?" said Carlisle, intent on his plate and not, thank goodness, on Grady's throat.

Mercury looked up. "I passed him while I was running, but that was about nine. Haven't seen him since. He was riding one of the lodge horses. Pass the little onions, please?"

He handed Mercury the onion bowl, and thought that if Mercury had been the one to put those "surprises" in his and Maggie's rooms, he was certainly as cool as a cucumber about finding them alive and well. And neither man seemed the least bit shocked—not even a tad irritated—to see Albatross returned in one piece.

To Mercury, Grady asked, "Where'd you see him?"

"Thanks." Mercury ladled some onions onto his plate. "Out on the Tranquility Trail."

Grady remembered seeing the Tranquility Trail on his map. He hadn't walked it, but as he remembered, it went in the opposite direction from the Tropical Isle Trail, heading off northeast through the woods and following a creek. He said, "You run every day?"

Chewing, Mercury nodded. He swallowed and added, "When the weather allows. It can be pretty goshdarned hot down Tombstone way. But it keeps me feeling young. Keeps me healthy."

"Bah," said Rance Carlisle.

Grady flicked his eyes to the left, for Carlisle was seated a distance from Mercury. Interesting. "Beg pardon, Carlisle?"

"Load of hogwash," Carlisle snorted. "Man lives in a natural state. You're destined to take sick and die, you do, and no amount of running all over hell and gone going to help that. Asinine notion. Me, I used to ride and rope with the Circle C boys—had to—but I quit as soon as I was able. These days, if I get the urge to jump on a horse and rope a calf, I just go take a nap till the feeling passes." He laughed at his own joke, then helped himself to more sausage and potatoes.

Mercury frowned, but said, "To each his own," and turned his concentration to his venison.

Grady, reaching for the bread, changed the subject. "You ever get your shark, Carlisle?"

The big man scowled. "No. But that reminds me. We have unfinished business, Maguire. I don't know what kind of trick you and that little gal played on me down at the cove, but I intend to finish with you before the day's out."

Threats. How tiresome. Grady leaned back in his chair, cocked an eyebrow—rather jauntily, he thought—and said, "Careful, Carlisle. I have a dull fork in my hand, you know."

Mercury snorted, but Carlisle, having not one shred of a sense of humor (a trait which Grady found even more dreary than the possibility that the man was a multiple murderer), growled, "Any time you're ready, Maguire."

"Never mind," said Grady, with a sigh turning back to

his lunch. You couldn't verbally fence with an unarmed man.

At least Mrs. Friar had been glad to see him, he thought, as he began to build a venison sandwich. She'd made off with Albatross, but not before she actually kissed him on the cheek. She'd cried at the reunion. Touching, really, how fond she was of that cat.

But now Gus hadn't shown up for lunch. It was a worrisome thing, because he liked Gus, or whatever his name was. He hated to think of him out there, somewhere, shot or stabbed or worse. But he couldn't mention it, not in front of these two.

Actually, he couldn't think of another blasted thing to say. A picture came into his mind of Gus, impaled on a wooden stake somewhere out there in the woods, and he nearly gagged on his sandwich. He put it on his plate again, eyeing it warily.

He wished Maggie would come down.

Mrs. Friar entered the dining room just then, carrying two bowls. She walked directly toward him, pulled an empty salad plate next to his place setting, and spooned an enormous amount of vanilla ice cream onto it, followed by an impressive quantity of raspberry syrup which was positively rife with whole, plump berries.

"My goodness!" said Grady as the housekeeper wordlessly left the table.

"What about the rest of us?" asked Carlisle, obviously irritated.

Mrs. Friar turned long enough to say, "You rescue my little Alby, then you get ice cream. You didn't even look for him 'cause you were too busy tryin' to wing that damn killer fish. The rest'a this is for *Miss* Maguire."

"By God!" breathed Carlisle, turning a nice shade of pink, Grady thought, as he watched the door swing closed behind her. Then louder, "I'll have your job, you back-talkin' old crow!"

"Welcome to it," came her voice, from the kitchen.

Mercury looked past Grady's shoulder, out the window. "Here's Gus now," he said, with something Grady could only take to be relief, and then returned to cutting his meat.

Maggie slid the last pin into her hair, checked one final time to make sure her skirts were in order, and then stepped into the hall and locked the door behind her. Not that it would do any good: Warden had let himself in before and he'd likely do it again.

She'd checked every door and drawer and cabinet before she'd opened it, and even then stood to the side, just in case they were rigged to blow up or launch knives or bullets or something. But everything had been safe. Well, untampered with, anyway.

There were things she hadn't checked too, but why go to all that trouble when she'd just have to check them again before she went to bed?

If she lived that long.

Amazing that Grady wasn't more jumpy, she thought as she turned the corner into the main hallway. Just in time to see someone go into Temperance Kellogg's room. Just the hem of a skirt.

Temperance? she wondered, just half a heartbeat before she heard a crash and a scream, and saw Mrs. Friar backing from the room, hands over her mouth.

Maggie was at her side in an instant, just in time for Mrs. Friar to double over and throw up all over both their hems.

With a grimace, Maggie pulled the housekeeper to the side, leaned her against the paneling, shook her own hem as clean as she could, and then crossed the hall to Temperance Kellogg's open door.

At first it just looked like a bright and sunny room. Empty, but cheerful. Maggie put out a hand and slowly opened the door wider. She stopped before it came to a rest against the wall.

There, to her left, Temperance Kellogg's body was slumped over a writing desk.

The pen was in its place beside the inkwell, which had been closed. The body was seated comfortably, and it might have been a peaceful, even blissful picture—Temperance, falling asleep at her work—except for the pool of blood under her head.

Maggie stepped around Mrs. Friar's tray and broken china and went closer. There were no signs of breathing.

She touched Temperance's hand. Still a little warm. She'd been dead for at least three-quarters of an hour, Maggie thought, a theory borne out by the pool of blood, which, upon closer inspection, was thick and dark, the drying edges turned brown.

A small whimper, coming from the hall, caught her attention, and she called, "Everything all right, Mrs. Friar?"

"Nothing's right," came the faint reply. "Everybody's gettin' killed."

A little crabbier. Good.

Maggie took hold of Temperance's hair and gently raised the head, saying loudly, "When you feel up to it, could you call my cousin, please?"

Just as she'd feared. The spindle had been shoved into Temperance's eye socket. Or perhaps Temperance's eye socket has been thrust down on the spindle. The end result was the same, anyway. She eased the head back down on the table, but not before she removed the bloody sheet of paper it had rested on.

Blotting the paper gingerly with her handkerchief, she turned toward the open door and said, "Mrs. Friar? Have you gone yet?"

"No," came the answer, after a pause. "You don't want me to come in there, do you?"

"No," said Maggie. "Before you go to call Grady, could you tell me about your Edison? When did you get it?"

Another pause. Then, "You mean the talkin' machine?"

"Yes." Maggie could almost read the paper, now. It appeared to be the last page of a manuscript.

"It just come over on the boat the day before you did. Don't know who sent it."

"You don't know?" Somebody was living happily ever after, as best as she could make out. The ink was smeared, completely obscured in places. "Wasn't there a note? A return address?"

"Note?" came Mrs. Friar's voice. She sounded more like herself now. "Just said, 'A gift to the Wapiti Lodge, from a friend.' Somethin' like that. No return address. Can I go now?"

Maggie looked up from the paper and slowly began to absorb the rest of the room in detail. "Did you play it?"

"Hell, no! Them mechanical things scare me." There was a moment of silence from the hall. "Why?"

"Did Mrs. Kellogg usually keep her door locked?" said Maggie, giving no explanation.

"Are you joking? Of course she did! When she didn't answer my knock, I tried the knob. It was open."

"All right," said Maggie. "You can go get Grady, now."

There was the sound of a sigh, then the housekeeper's fading footsteps.

Maggie turned her full attention to the room. No signs of a struggle, no vases or furniture smashed, no pictures knocked down. Not even a crooked picture. No, there had been no struggle. Temperance had known her killer, known him well enough to let him in. Well enough that she had turned her back on him.

Maggie put the paper on a part of the desk that was clear of blood, and found the bathroom. She discarded her handkerchief in the wastebasket—it'd never come clean now—and rinsed her hands at the sink. Nothing out of the ordinary in the bathroom, either.

She peeked into the medicine cabinet. The usual traveler's toiletry items, all neat and tidy. Roman's shaving things, set to the side. Temperance's things, lined up in a neat row along the back of the vanity. Soap, toilet water, all the usual paraphernalia, except for a bottle of laudanum, two-thirds gone.

Maggie dried her hands, then picked up the laudanum, opened it, and sniffed. "Hm," she said, capping the bottle again. Now, why would Temperance be taking opium?

On a hunch, she bent to the wastebasket and lifted her bloody handkerchief off the top. Another bottle, this one empty. A brief prowl through the bathroom cabinets yielded two more bottles, unopened.

Temperance had come prepared. It was obvious, from the amount consumed, that this was a habit of long standing. No wonder she spent most of her time in her room, and always looked so pale. What had appeared at first to be reticence of manner and a general air of unwellness was now explained. It was a miracle she could write at all, in her condition.

But then, Maggie thought, perhaps it helped concentration. Absently, she turned on the tap, lifted her shirt, and began to scrub at the last bit of Mrs. Friar's sick.

Didn't opium smokers report a clarity of thought, she wondered, a brightness of the dream state? Of course, they were drugged to the gills and couldn't move, but then, perhaps all Temperance did was sit and write and drink laudanum, then sit and write some more until she fell asleep.

Her skirt was as clean as she was going to get it. She turned off the tap, then stopped in the doorway, leaning against the frame. Staring at Temperance's body, she crossed her arms. She wondered which had come first: Roman or the opium.

She had a feeling it was Roman.

TWENTY-FOUR

GRADY EXCUSED HIMSELF AND WALKED TOWARD THE stairs at a normal pace. Wouldn't do to upset everybody—well, Gus, Carlisle, and Mercury were the only ones left to upset—and Mrs. Friar had at least owned the sense to whisper the bad news about Mrs. Kellogg into his ear.

And Maggie had thought Mrs. Kellogg was the smart one, staying locked in her room.

Walking around a small spattering of foreign material which he could only take to be vomit, he reached the Kelloggs' room, and found Maggie, sitting on the bed, reading. "Nice you can be so calm," he said. "Who threw up out in the—"

His eye lit, just then, on Temperance's body. With an arched brow (and a slight quivering in his stomach of ice cream and berries) he took in the blood, looked quickly away, and said, "Maggie?"

"What?" She looked up. "Oh. Spindle through the eye. A mean sort of crime. But then, did we expect anything less?"

Grady looked around the room. Everything was meticulous. Odd. Odder still that Maggie should be sitting calmly at the death scene, reading. He avoided looking at the body again, and wished he hadn't eaten quite so heartily. He said, "No struggle?"

Maggie turned over another page. "Doesn't appear to have been."

Grady turned and checked the latch on the hall door. No scratches in the brass or the wood. He looked back, toward Maggie. "She let him in?"

"Appears that way." Maggie slowly riffled through the top pages of what he now recognized as a manuscript. How could she be so damnably calm? Oh, he was used to the knife-throwing, the juggling. He could even deal with her standing on her head once in a blue moon. But *reading*?

She looked up, then, giving her head a slow shake, and said, "Mrs. Kellogg certainly was tidy for an opium addict."

"Opium?" he asked, somewhat carefully. Maggie, his dear, sweet Maggie, had finally flipped her bonnet. Mrs. Kellogg, an opium smoker? He sniffed the air, and found no trace of the drug's sickly perfume. The stress of the situation had pushed Maggie over the edge, that was it. She'd needed this vacation more than he realized. Not that it was a vacation anymore, not by any means. Why, if he'd only known, he wouldn't have been such a ninny; wouldn't have been so hard to pry out of town that she and Otto had to make up that story about Edison.

Edison! He'd been angry about that, and suddenly he was angry all over again. Well, not angry, perhaps, but most certainly annoyed. Of all the—

And then he remembered his cousin, his only living relative, who was sitting cross-legged in the middle of a four-poster bed—reading!—and not fifteen feet from a dead body, and that she had very probably gone mad as a bug. Oh, if he'd only known, he would have packed the four of them—Otto and Ozzie, too—off to someplace soothing, someplace exotic, someplace very far away.

She must have read the look on his face, because she suddenly rolled her eyes and said, "Grady, honestly. Stop thinking I've gone mad—or whatever is rolling around in that mind of yours—and go look in the bathroom. Empty bottle in the wastebasket, a partial on the vanity, and two full ones on the shelf. Anybody who goes through dope that fast either has a taste for it, or they've just had a leg amputated. And Mrs. Kellogg seems to have both her lower limbs intact."

Grady sighed, as much in resignation as relief. So much for that theory. He said, "I'll take your word for it." Pointing, he added, "Is that Temperance and Roman's latest opus?"

Maggie nodded. She set the top part of the manuscript aside, and began to quickly peruse the next pages. "Look through the wastebasket, would you? The one beside the desk. See if you can find another title page." Without looking up, she waved a sheet of paper at him. He couldn't read it, but it was primarily blank, with a few lines of writing centered about a third of the way down the page.

Carefully averting his eyes, he went to the desk, removed the wastebasket, and then removed himself a respectful distance from the body before he sat down and started to search.

Peering into the basket, he remarked. "I've never seen such organized litter! You know, you could take a lesson from this."

Maggie, immersed in reading, grunted.

Cast off sheets, six or eight or ten to a packet, were folded precisely into quarters and pierced in the center. Probably by the spindle, he thought, and then shuddered. He hadn't gone through half the pile when he spied the paper he was looking for.

"Found it," he said, straightening the sheet over his knee. He read aloud, "*Mesa Mike in Indian Country: The Littlest Squaw.*"

Maggie, who had set aside another handful of papers, held up hers. "And I've got the revised title. *Mesa Mike at the Ghost Lodge: Salty Bob's Revenge.*"

Grady furrowed his brow. "Doesn't even sound like the same story."

"It isn't." Maggie moved the last of the papers onto her lap. "I'm just skimming, mind, but it seems to me that this book starts out in a Paiute camp, and then all of a sudden switches gears to a ghost town. Mesa Mike, who's supposed to be the hero, just disappears. I don't mean by any supernatural means, I mean that it looks like she just forgot to write him in. It's mostly about a character named Avis, who Salty Bob Waters is out to get. But there are other travelers stranded in this ghost town, too, and he's also out to get them. Sound familiar?"

Grady leaned back in his chair. The story was just a little too true to life for his liking. He said, "Go on."

"In a minute." Maggie started turning pages again. Flip, flip, flip. He should have been the one to read it, he thought. He might have been slower, but at least he would have remembered exactly what he read.

After a few minutes of picking the lint off his socks to pass the time, Maggie said to him, "Anyone seem surprised to see the kitty?" Still intent on the page, she didn't look up at him.

"No," he said, to the top of her head. "Nobody except Mrs. Friar. She brought me a sweet." He smiled.

Maggie grunted and turned another page over. "Did Gus ever come back?"

"As a matter of fact, he did," Grady said, somewhat jauntily.

Maggie's head popped up. "Really?"

Grady nodded.

Maggie smiled, just a little. "Good," she said, then went back to reading.

Five minutes passed, then ten, then fifteen, and Grady was about to sneak out and go back downstairs when Maggie turned over the last of the manuscript.

"Well!" she said, standing up and straightening her skirts. "There's a small part of the mystery solved, at any rate. I think we'll go down and beard our three lions in the den. Or the game room. Maybe we should all take a listen at the Edison.'' One corner of her mouth turned up, she marched past him and out into the hall.

He knew better than to ask her what she was thinking. He could practically hear the gears turning as it was. Closing the door behind him, he followed her down the stairs, through the empty lobby, and into the dining room.

The only person there was Mrs. Friar, busily clearing the dishes.

''Make it stop,'' said Maggie in disgust. The Edison's message hadn't been changed, and she still couldn't identify the voice.

Grady ceased cranking, and as Maggie walked past him, toward the window, she saw him give the trumpet a respectful swipe with his handkerchief.

She felt terrible. Terrible for tricking him to get him here. He could have been safely pouting over Miriam Cosgrove back in San Francisco. But, she reminded herself, she would have been, well, dead. If it hadn't been for Grady, that tricked-up knife under her bed would have found her for certain.

Folding her arms behind her back, she stared out the window. No sign of anyone. Carlisle wasn't even taking pot shots at the shark. Why, in bluc blazes, did they have to go cavorting all over the landscape when they knew four people had died?

Well, thcy only knew about three of them, she reminded herself. All except the real Sam Warden.

And what was she missing? There had to be a hint, a clue, something! Something she'd missed, something that was going to result in more murders. And they'd be her fault, just as surely as Phoebe's death, and Roman Kellogg's and Temperance's had been.

She felt sick, and put a hand over her stomach. She realized it had been gnawing at her since she found Mr. Andrews, and the fact that she couldn't have drawn anything from that killing earlier—at least nothing that would have prevented the others—did little to comfort her.

She always tried to be logical about these things, to stay levelheaded and calm. But this time, it was hitting too close to home, and was coming too fast. This time, her life was in danger, and Grady's. She was just beginning to take in the reality of it. The imminence of death was not something that could be long pushed aside, although she'd managed for over a day.

She frowned, eyes on the cove. Well, it certainly looked peaceful today. Those idiots! She'd planned to just lock them in a room together until tomorrow. Now three of them—five, if you counted Grady and herself—were in mortal danger. And a killer was free and roaming among them.

"Mags?"

She turned to find Grady regarding her curiously.

He said, "You all right? You're awfully quiet."

She took her eyes off the cove and moved to sit opposite him, leaning forward, elbows on her knees. "Grady," she began, "I'm sorry. I'm really sorry. We tricked you into coming on a vacation, and it's all turned out so . . . so . . ."

He reached across and took her hand, smiling. "Well, Maggie m'girl," he said kindly, "what's life without a few disasters?"

Despite herself, she broke out in a grin. Reading her mind again, was he? She said, "You sounded like Papa, just then."

"Dear Uncle Custus," Grady said, and tickled her palm. "Was he invited to a great many murder parties, then?"

Laughing, Maggie slid her hand away and leaned back into her chair. "Honestly, Grady! You know what I mean." Her smile dropped away abruptly then, and she added, "If only I had a clue!"

Grady took off his spectacles and began to polish them. "You've got to follow your own advice, Mags. 'Start from the beginning,' that what you're always saying to me. Besides, I thought Mrs. Kellogg solved it for you. In the manuscript."

She shook her head. "Only part of it. One murder." Grady looked puzzled, and then she remembered that in her excitement—brief though it had been—she hadn't told him. "In the manuscript," she explained, "Avis, who I'm pretty certain was the fictional version of Mrs. Kellogg, figures out that one of the other guests, a Bat Swober, is an—"

"Bat *Swober*?" interrupted Grady. His handkerchief had gone back into his pocket and his gold-rimmed spectacles were once again perched on his nose.

Maggie shrugged. "I never said she was a *great* writer. Anyway, she determines that Bat Swober is an anagram for Salty Bob Waters. Without the 'Salty,' of course. And, as we know, he was the Kelloggs' version of Sam Warden. I'm wondering about Temperance, because the fictional Avis had a rather seedy affair with Salty Bob some years earlier."

She paused, tapping her chin. "Well, anyway, she sneaks into his room late at night and stabs him through the heart. He never wakes up."

Grady raised an eyebrow. "And?"

"Well, the next day, when Avis's husband is killed by a fake Apache arrow, she—"

"Sorry Mags," Grady cut in, both brows lifted this time, "but a fake Apache arrow?"

She sighed. "I didn't write it, all right? Anyway, our Avis discovers the hard way that she's killed the wrong man, and . . ."

Abruptly, she stopped and jumped to her feet, for she heard a sound that iced her veins. She turned toward the window just in time to see a riderless horse, reins flapping, gallop across the front lawn and turn toward the barn.

Grady had heard it, too, for he was already out of his chair.

"Gus?" she asked, as they both started for the front door.

"Afraid so," replied Grady, right on her heels as she opened the screen and raced, skirts hiked, after the horse.

TWENTY-FIVE

SHE DIDN'T BOTHER TO SADDLE A FRESH MOUNT. AT a glance, she knew the riderless chestnut that had thundered into the barn was fit to ride, and she grabbed the horn with one hand and swung herself up and into the saddle.

"How the hell do you do that without using the stirrup?" Grady asked, and before she had time to answer, he added, "Don't tell me. That Mexican trick rider with Daddy's circus."

"Pablo DeGarza," she said, patting at her skirt pockets. "And he was Scottish." She heaved a small sigh of relief when she felt the outline of her Colt. Gathering her reins, she said, "Grady, if you could just bring yourself to—"

He took a step away and stubbornly crossed his arms. "I am *not* getting on a horse. Then why did he have a Mexican name?"

She pursed her lips, then decided this wasn't the time to argue with him about learning to ride. Or Pablo DeGarza. She said, "Crimeny, Grady, does it matter now? Just follow me, all right?"

Without waiting for a reply, she crouched and leaned forward and cried, *"Hiya!"* with all her might.

Nothing happened.

She sat up again. "Rental horse," she grumbled. "I should have known."

Grady stepped forward and, very fortunately for him, he didn't laugh. All he said was, "Duck," and then, open-handed, he slapped the horse on its rear as hard as he could.

Maggie crouched just in time to avoid banging her head on the barn doorframe, and then she was in the clear, galloping back toward the path from which the horse had emerged.

Up the trail she went, hauling the horse back into a lope so that she could make out the tracks it had left when it was coming the other way. At the fork between the Tropical Isle and Majestic View trails, she followed the track back into the trees, along the Majestic View.

The trail came out of the forest almost as soon as it had entered it, and cut around a large open area—trees to the left of the trail, rolling pasture land to the right. Gus still wasn't in sight, and she urged the horse back into a gallop until she passed the meadow and the trail was canopied by trees again.

And there, at the top of a rise, she saw him.

She thought he was dead at first. Who wouldn't believe it of a man, hanged by the neck from an ancient sycamore? As she got nearer, she saw a leg move, but passed it off as a reflex. Sometimes, bodies would twitch intermittently for fifteen minutes, sometimes longer.

But as she came within fifty feet, she saw that Gus had a hand caught between the rope and his neck, and that he was fighting to breathe.

She sank her heels into the horse for the last spurt forward, then reined him in beside the dangling Gus and swung his body into the saddle, atop her lap. Immediately, there was slack in the rope. She knew immediately that he'd been hanged from horseback, and also, that he was in terrible shape. His face—and his fingers, where they were caught in the noose—were bright purple, and the rope cut into his neck cruelly.

She tugged at the knot, finally loosening it, and pulled the noose from around his neck. Neither was an easy task, for his body was a limp and slippery as a dead fish—a very large and bony dead fish. But the rope came off at last, and he flopped back into her arms and knocked them both off the horse.

She struggled out from under him and grabbed the horse's reins just in time to prevent another runaway, and then she knelt beside Gus.

He was breathing: big, rattling breaths. His eyes were pressed shut, although she couldn't tell if it was because he was concentrating so hard on breathing, or because he'd passed out.

Rubbing his swollen and purple fingers, and thanking God that she had finally—finally!—saved *somebody*, she said, "Gus! Gus, do you hear me?"

His lips moved, although no sound came out. She lowered her ear to his mouth. The hoarse whisper was still hard to understand. "Thank you," was what he was saying.

She sat up again. "You're welcome, Gus," she said, near to tears. "Can you move your fingers?"

He crooked them slightly. Just a small gesture, but it let her know the nerve endings weren't damaged. They were still swollen, but the purple was fading a little.

"Gus, who did this to you?"

She lowered her head to his in time to hear him rasp, "Didn't . . . see."

"Not even a shirttail? Nothing?"

Eyes still closed, he shook his head, then grimaced.

Now what? She'd gotten to him in time. That was enough of a miracle, she supposed, but it would have been nice if he'd seen his assailant. Even a glimpse of a shoe, even the *toe* of a shoe, would have been a good deal more information than she already had! The stupid little con artist! Why hadn't he kept his eyes open?

And then she caught herself at it—getting all riled up at Gus when she was the one who was supposed to be finding all the answers, of whom it was *expected*, for goodness sake—and she shut down her anger.

"Lie still," she said, more gently than even she had planned, "and I'll look for some water."

She stood up and looked over the saddle. Nothing. Gus would just have to do without until she got him back to the lodge.

At least he was out of the running. Sam Warden might do a great many things, all of them evil, but hanging himself to throw her off the scent was going too far. After all, how would he have known the horse would run straight back to the lodge? And even if it did, how would he know someone would see it come in?

No, it was too far-fetched, even for her grasping mind, which at this moment, was willing to accept almost anything as a clue.

"All right, Gus," she said, turning. "Let's get you up and on this nag, all right?"

Dumbly, he nodded and tried to sit up. He made it so far as to prop himself on an elbow, then fell back, mouthing, "Can't."

"I'll help," she said, and tied the horse to a tree before she knelt behind Gus, arms under his shoulders. Where was that blasted Grady when you needed him?

At last Gus was on his feet, or a reasonable facsimile thereof, and she got him over the horse and place his hands on the saddle horn.

"I'm going to push now. You ready?"

Gus nodded, just a little.

Shoulder under his backside, she heaved him toward the saddle. He managed to swing a leg over, though he remained hunched over and gripping the horn tightly. He turned toward her—turned his whole body, she noticed, rather than turn his poor neck—and mouthed the word, "Strong," at her.

She was about to reply that yes she was, when she heard someone whistling. She burst into a grin and turned back the way she'd come, ready to tell Grady that he must have run all the way, but there was no one there. The sound was coming from behind her, on the other side of the hill.

She wheeled just in time to see Mercury Marchand's head bobbing over the rise. As much as she had suspected him—and everyone else—she felt the bottom drop out of her stomach as she pulled the pistol from her pocket and hid it behind her back.

He waved, smiling wide, and called, "Hullo!"

"Good afternoon," she answered as he drew nearer. She wished Grady would hurry, although common sense told her that he couldn't be much closer than the split in the path.

He was ten feet away when he stopped, looked at the slumped Gus curiously, and then, his eyes darting suspiciously to Maggie, to Gus, then back again, said, "What's happened here? Is he all right?" Just then he must have seen the rope. He gasped just a little—too little for Maggie to tell whether it was in genuine surprise, or frustrationn over a plan gone wrong—and added, rather nervously, "W-what's going on?"

Maggie pulled the Colt from behind her back and aimed it straight at his belly. "We're all going to walk back to the lodge, that's what's going on." She wiggled the barrel slightly. "Out in front, if you wouldn't mind?"

Slowly, and with a look of shock on his face, he stepped past her.

"Stop there," she said. He didn't look like he was armed, but you never could tell. Throwing the reins to Gus with a "Stay put," she moved close behind Mercury and pressed the barrel of the gun against his ear.

"Hands over your head, please," she said, and when he complied, began to pat down his tailored clothing, one-handed.

"Maggie, Miss Maguire, please! I never—"

"Quiet," she hissed, and moved the gun to the middle of his back while she felt his legs. No knife in the boot. No blade or pocket gun in his waistband, or hidden under his shirt. Drat! Why couldn't this be easy?

She backed up, easing the gun away from his body but still holding it level, and said, "All right. You can put your arms down now."

He lowered them slowly, then turned partway around. "Why are you doing this, Maggie? I never—"

"Quiet!" she snapped. "And turn around again."

She'd get this crew back to the Wapiti, and then she'd think. She hadn't had time to think all week—no, it had been little more than forty-eight hours! No wonder she was so fuddled. Sam Warden had thrown her timing off, that was all. Mercury had thrown her timing off.

"All right, Gus," she said, reaching back to take his reins. "Let's get going."

She fell to her knees and clamped her hands to her ears as the blast went off. Mercury crumpled to the ground.

Above her, hanging on to the saddle one-handed, Gus held a smoking Remington. He reholstered it, then fell forward onto the horse's neck.

"Try to hang me, will he?" were the last words he croaked before he passed out.

TWENTY-SIX

AFTER RUNNING HEADLONG INTO MRS. FRIAR AND briefly explaining what little he knew of what was going on, and not-so-briefly getting her calmed down again, Grady followed Maggie's tracks up the trail. It was hot and there were too many bugs, and he had just about decided that if Sam Warden wanted to kill him, so be it. At least he wouldn't have to fight mosquitos and chiggers and those green leafy-winged things, of which he had swatted six at last count.

Just as he was wiping the blood off his hand—from another swatted mosquito—he came upon the fork between the Majestic View and the Tropical Isle trails. He also came upon Carlisle. The man was sitting on the ground with his hands wrapped round his knees—a stretch over his big belly. His head was down.

"Carlisle?" said Grady, wary as much as worried. "Are you all right, old man?" He fumbled in his pocket for the short-nosed Colt, and thought for the umpteenth time that he really should get a holster for it.

Carlisle moaned softly just as Grady found his gun. He kept his hand in his pocket, however, and held his ground. "Carlisle? Can you speak?"

Relative silence. No sounds but those of nature, and Carlisle's labored breathing. Grady took a deep breath, filled his cheeks, and blew it out. He should go to Carlisle and help him. But then, if he did that, Carlisle might just leap up and sink a knife into his belly.

Maggie might be on her way back already. On the other hand, she could be sitting up there in the forest, waiting for him and tapping her foot. Or she could be in danger.

He regarded Carlisle again. There was no change. He said, "Is it your heart, old man?"

A small nod.

"Did you take your medicine?"

Again, the nod.

Damn! He knew what he *should* do. He should leave Carlisle behind and run up the path after Maggie's horse, and watch his back. Or then again, on strictly humanitarian grounds, he should go to Carlisle and help him up and back to the lodge, if he could walk. What the hell was he doing all the way out here, anyway, with that supposed bum ticker of his?

Hunting people?

It was a sobering thought, and he was about to cut a large circle past Carlisle and run after Maggie, when he stopped. If Carlisle wasn't really suffering, he could shoot him in the back as he passed. Why, he might be lying in wait for Maggie, too!

"All right, chum," Grady said, moving toward him. "Let's get you up."

But instead of approaching from the front, he circled behind. "Sorry about this," he said, and cracked Carlisle over the skull with the butt of his pistol.

Carlisle held steady for a moment, then fell to the side.

"By God!" Grady said, pocketing his pistol again, then mopping at his brow. This heat was really annoying. "That'll hold you for a bit. And now . . ." He bent to the sprawled figure, and immediately, his clever ex-pickpocket fingers found the pill vial and drew it out. Stuffing the vial in his own pocket for the moment, he quickly frisked Carlisle and frowned. He was unarmed.

Now, that was nerve for you! If he happened to be the

killer, you'd think he would have been better prepared. And if he wasn't Sam Warden, you'd think he'd want to protect himself!

Grady sighed. He'd never understand why some people did the things they did, and now he'd knocked a man unconscious for nothing. Although, he noted, Carlisle's face didn't seem red. Not even pink.

Frowning, Grady again reached for the pills. He studied the label. Except for Carlisle's name and TAKE AS NEEDED written in blurry blue ink, it told him nothing. He unscrewed the lid and this time, shook one into his palm.

He sniffed it. It didn't smell like anything in particular. How could you tell with a pill, anyway?

He stuck the vial back in Carlisle's inside pocket and stood up. What did they put in heart pills? Was it poisonous? He kicked himself for not knowing, for never having developed an interest in medicine. If he'd read anything about it, he would have remembered, even if it had been ten years ago.

He had, he thought rather smugly, as he moved away from Carlisle and up the Majestic View Trail, that kind of a mind. And pushing himself into a sort of jog, he moved along, rolling the pill between his fingers and wondering if he should just swallow it and see.

Maggie trudged back down the trail, leading the horse. It trailed behind her with its head low, probably because it had a double burden—the roped-into-place Gus and, behind him, Mercury.

Gus had only been able to wing Mercury in the arm, after all. Shocking that a grown man would faint from a little thing like that. But then, she'd seen grown men faint as a result of much less trauma.

She snorted. She'd like to see one of them go through childbirth, or just the curse. Even a full day of canning peaches. Now *that* would be funny!

She twisted her head back. They were both still out cold,

which was good because it gave her time to think. She needed to get her bearings. Actually, she needed to toss knives or juggle, but having nothing at hand, she settled for the rhythm of her shoes and those of the horse.

She decided that she'd best take Grady's advice—and her own—and start from the beginning, right from the time they stepped onto the dock. But somehow she started thinking about Sam Warden, and what a mess he'd made of the vacation. Or what a mess they'd all made of it for him.

Obviously, there'd been some plan made with Mr. Andrews. Maybe Warden had told him he was playing a joke on some friends, and that he was the stand-in. Perhaps it had been more ominous. But the fact was that Temperance Kellogg had stabbed Andrews—Warden's red herring—and thrown his well-timed plan for a loop.

So, right from that first morning, he was winging it.

He might have started with a script of the week, with the murders in a specific order and by a specific means, but that was no longer the case.

Why, look at poor Phoebe! That shark could have gotten any one of them. It just happened to get her. Sheer bad luck.

And Kellogg? Nothing neat and tidy about an axe in the back, nothing at all. And yet, Warden had set those nooses she and Grady and Albatross had blundered into days, perhaps weeks, in advance. No, she corrected herself, Albatross hadn't blundered into them. He'd been taken and hung up there for bait.

Despite the heat, she broke out in gooseflesh. Strange that the abuse of a poor, dumb creature should affect her more than a handful of murders, but there you were.

Rubbing at her arms, she got her mind back to the business at hand. Temperance Kellogg, for instance. There had been nothing clever or witty about that murder. He'd just walked in, said howdy-do, and killed her.

Maggie supposed the laudanum had had something to do with it. That, or perhaps Temperance was feeling so wretched over her part in Andrews's death that she simply let Warden in, knowing he was going to kill her. Perhaps she considered it justice of a sort.

Grady's snake? He would've had to have brought that with him, as well as that gizmo under her own bed. Those were planned in advance. But hanging Gus? A rope dropped hastily from a tree limb? That was a last minute idea if ever she'd seen one.

Whatever plan Sam Warden had made for an entertaining weekend—well, *his* idea of entertaining, anyway—had gone out the window with Mr. Andrews. Even those recordings on the Edison (and she had every cause to believe that he'd sent it to the lodge) had been choppy, uneven. One before the murders started, one after the third murder, and not a peep since.

She clucked her tongue aloud, startling the horse. Without breaking stride, she patted him on the neck, and thought how disappointed Sam must be to see his plans going so awry. She and Grady had escaped, unpunctured by blade or fang. They'd disarmed his trap in the forest. What was the plan to be then, she wondered. Would he have dropped by later on and finished them off with a machete or a club as they hung upside down and helpless? Well, they'd foiled that, and they'd rescued the cat while they were at it. And just now she'd saved Gus's skin.

Suddenly, things didn't appear to be going Sam Warden's way. She realized they'd been falling apart ever since that first morning, when she'd found Andrews' body. Right from the beginning.

Of course, they hadn't fallen apart nearly enough.

Half their party was dead, no thanks to her.

Mercury was coming around when she spied Grady walking toward her. Mercury groaned, and then she heard him say clearly, "Shot! I've been shot!"

"Yes, you have," she replied, leading the horse in Grady's direction. The distance between them was diminishing rapidly. ''Don't worry,'' she added, as an afterthought. ''It's not fatal.''

''Why am I tied to this horse? Next to . . . Now I remember!'' Panic leapt, rather then crept, into Mercury's voice. ''Why've you got me tied up next to a killer?''

Maggie sighed. ''Don't be crabby.'' Really, it was rather disconcerting, talking to the seat of Mercury's pants rather than to his face. She supposed she should have tied him the other way round. ''It was the only way I could get you both back to civilization,'' she went on. ''In one trip, that is.''

Gus chose that moment to groan, and Maggie sighed again. It didn't rain but what it poured. Mercury cried, ''Get me off'a here! Get me away from this maniac before he comes to!'' Just then Grady walked up.

Maggie stopped the horse, saying to Mercury's pants, ''He can't hurt you. I've got his gun.'' Then, ''Hello, Grady.''

Grady stopped about five feet away and propped his hands on his hips. He pursed his lips, looked at Maggie, then looked at the horse and its cargo, then back at Maggie again. He reached into his pocket and brought out his handkerchief while taking off his spectacles, and then, studiously, began to rub at the lenses.

''Been busy, I see,'' he said calmly, holding a lens up to the sun, then polishing it again. ''You plan to take everyone into custody until the boat comes?''

There was nothing more annoying than a smug cousin, particularly one who was polishing his lenses. Maggie led the horse forward, right into him so that he had to step to the other side of the animal, and kept walking.

''Grady!'' she heard Mercury cry out. ''Grady, he tried to kill me! Get me down!''

''Who tried to kill you? Gus?'' Grady answered.

''Get me down!''

Maggie heard Grady say, ''Well, old man, if you're

roped into place up there, it must be for a good reason." She smiled.

"But Grady!"

Then Gus moaned again and croaked, "Help! Help me!"

Maggie chirped, "Quiet, both of you," just as Grady, who had circled around behind the horse, came up next to her.

"Might I ask why?" Grady said, stepping into pace alongside her.

"Why they're tied to the horse, or why Gus can't talk too well, or where I got the rope, or—"

"Where *did* you get the rope?" interrupted Grady.

"Or why I think I know who the killer is?" Maggie finished.

"He is!" said both of the men tied to the horse.

Ignoring them, Grady said, "Yes," without a second's pause. "All of the above."

"First," she said, "did you see anyone on your way up?"

"Carlisle. He appeared to be having an attack. He was unarmed. Not even a knife. Oh! And I got one of his pills."

"Really?" she said, with a smile. "Those pickpocket skills—if a person can call them that—do come in handy every once in a while, Grady."

"Well, not exactly," he said, watching his feet. "I sort of . . . well, I bashed him over the head first."

Maggie managed to hold back the laugh that came bubbling up her throat, and turned it into a cough and an arched a brow. "Oh?"

Grady glared at her. "It was either that or take a chance on a knife in the back."

"Let me off of here!" wailed Mercury.

"Get me away from this killer!" rasped Gus.

"Both of you, be quiet," Maggie said sternly. A niggling feeling deep in her gut suddenly blossomed and traveled upward, into her head, where it ended as a sensation of light-headed jubilance. Right from the beginning, right where she should have started! At last! "Grady? Can I see the pill?"

He dug into his pocket, produced it, and handed it to her. It was small and white and round. She sniffed it. No odor. She popped it in her mouth and crunched down.

"Maggie!" Grady cried, grabbing for the horse's reins. "For God's sake, spit it out!"

"What! What's she doing?" cried Mercury, who was facing the other way.

"What's goin' on?" Gus echoed, although somewhat more hoarsely.

Maggie continued to chew. She feared she was grinning like a fool, but made no attempt to stop it. "I'm hungry, that's all. I missed lunch."

Grady took her by the shoulders and gave her a shake. "But Maggie—"

"Sugar," she said, the grin bursting into a bubble of laughter, and pushed his hands away. Something physical, to keep that bubble from turning into the hysterics of relief. "Just a sugar pill." She took the reins back from him and started walking again.

Grady was mopping his brow. "My Lord, Maggie. Don't scare me like that again! How did you know it was sugar?"

Under control again, she shrugged. "I didn't. I had a pretty fair idea, though." Grady looked daggers at her, and she put a hand on his arm. "Now, don't get all heated up, Grady. That's why I chewed it. If it had tasted at all like medicine, I would have spat it out right away."

She had to stop then, because within their ropes, Mercury and Gus had gotten into a shoving match of sorts. "Good gravy," she groaned under her breath. "Now, nobody tried to kill anybody else, all right?"

"Are you crazy?" came Mercury's voice. "He *shot* me!"

"Damn straight!" whispered Gus.

She went to work on the ropes. "Only because he

thought you tried to hang him,'' she said calmly. ''Say you didn't, Mercury.''

''What! I never did any such thing! I was just—''

''Not to me,'' Maggie said, drawing the rope through. ''To him.''

From the other side of the horse, Maggie heard him swear to Gus that he hadn't done it. And then Gus said, ''Well then, I'm right apologetic about shootin' you. I didn't get you bad, did I?''

Maggie pulled a knot free, and Mercury came sliding toward the ground. ''That's better,'' she said. Two more knots, and Gus slithered down, too.

Mercury studied the bandage on his arm. ''Nice job. Who packed this?''

''I did,'' said Maggie, and handed Gus back his gun.

Under his breath, Mercury grumped, ''You ruined my shirt though. Linen.''

Grady, who was holding the horse during all of this, said, ''I don't suppose anyone would mind if I asked just what the hell is going on?''

''Yes,'' said Maggie, ''they would. I'll tell you later. Now, gentlemen, we have a problem. Somewhere on the road up ahead is Rance Carlisle, also known as Sam Warden. Grady says that he didn't have a gun on him, but he's smart. He could have an arsenal hidden out in these woods for all I know, and we have to get past him.''

Well, they were all ears now. Three males, all rapt. She couldn't have done a better job of capturing their attention if she'd set her hair on fire.

''Of course,'' she went on, ''he has no reason to think we suspect him in particular. But then, he's running out of time. He thinks he has five people left to kill before tomorrow. And so, gentlemen, here's my plan.''

TWENTY-SEVEN

RANCE CARLISLE, ALIAS SAM WARDEN, CRAWLED UP from the ground and shook his head to coax some blood back into it. That bastard, Grady Maguire, had snuck up on him from behind, that's what he'd done. Another mistake! He'd been beset by them. Must be something in the stars, that was it. Mercury squaring Mars or something, or one of those retrograde things.

He made a mental note to add Madame Zelda to his victim list. She'd assured him that this particular week was prime for finishing up old business. Not that she had any idea what sort of business he was planning to finish up. Fat, stupid cow.

He stood up and ran his fingers through his hair, combing it into place, and then he patted his pockets. His wallet was still there, and his pills. Also his big belly. Madame Zelda wasn't the only fat old cow around. In the time since he'd swum out of that icy bay and crawled to civilization, he'd packed on eighty-five pounds. It was the best disguise ever, with no need for putty noses or false chins. Just a two-inch lift in the shoe and a little hair dye and a different meter to the voice, and even his own mother wouldn't have recognized him. Nosiree Bob, not Big Rance Carlisle, King of the Circle C.

He chuckled to himself as he walked fifteen feet up the path, then cut off into the weeds. A half-minute of searching, and his hand came up clutching the Winchester he'd stashed when he heard someone coming up the path. Another minute and he found the pistol he'd thrown and the little derringer. He'd only managed to duck into the trees when that Maguire girl came thundering by, but she was too intent on saving Gus to even scan the sides of the path.

He frowned. *Nosy little no-good bitch*, he thought as he walked back to the fork, then started up the Majestic View Trail. Time to finish them off, once and for all. Mercury, and those damned Maguires, both of them.

At least Gus—or should he say Rendell? Vance Middleton? Russ the Sheepman? Reuben Bartlett? There were so many names to pick from—was hanging from a tree, long dead.

That, at least, had gone right, and it had been so simple! A rock thrown to the back of the head to daze him, the noose thrown up into the tree, and then *wham!* Spook the horse out from underneath. Of course, the little bastard had come partway to his senses just before the last part, and stuck his hand under the rope.

Well, that shouldn't matter. *Con Man Choked by Own Hand!* the papers should say.

He laughed out loud before he caught himself and stopped, staring up the path. No one yet. No one to hear, no one to see. But he wouldn't let it happen again. He'd put his foot in it too many times already. No, check that. Temperance had thrown it all off. Damn her anyway! How dare she kill his handpicked actor! All right, a second-string actor, but *his* actor, nonetheless. The fact that he, himself, was going to eventually kill Andrews made little difference. He was supposed to be fifth in line: not first, but fifth. When the remaining guests were good and scared, his death was supposed to put them at ease.

I can't go on with this, his suicide note was supposed to have read. And it would be signed, *A. M. Andrews, alias Sam Warden.* And then that Maguire bitch was supposed to leap up and say, "By God, it's an anagram!" And then she and the cousin of hers would congratulate themselves and Temperance would come out of her room again—all the others, of course, being dead—and he would have finished them off.

The water moccasin for that spectacle-polishing, prissy smart-ass, Grady. The perfect death for him, to be found with his pants down in the water closet!

Miss-Maggie-Too-Smart-For-Her-Own-Good Maguire was to have been the last, and he'd had something special planned. Something with ropes and cool naked skin that would take place in his room. Maybe several times, before he killed her. Without thinking, he licked at his lips, then stopped himself abruptly.

No more. Oh well.

So he'd set Temperance's springblade for Maggie, instead. He'd originally planned to set it under Temperance's bed, and then *wham!* But she'd been so kind about letting him in, and the spindle through her eye had worked just as well, he supposed. Actually, it had really been more poetic. It just irritated him that things hadn't gone correctly. He didn't like it. It irritated him. He'd had to do everything out of order, or put the wrong people with the wrong deaths.

He was about halfway round the place where the path was open land on one side when he spied a speck, just turning into view at the top of the trees. Quickly, he ducked back into the trees at his left and stayed there until the speck grew into separate shapes. Maggie, leading the horse. And the horse had a body on it. Couldn't be anyone but the late, lamented Gus.

He smiled. Creeping back out onto the path, he sat down in a shady spot, leaving his Winchester an arm's length behind him in the brush. The pistol was in his hand, the derringer in its sheath.

Odd that Grady wasn't with her, he thought as he lowered his head, assuming the posture of a man who's just had a serious attack of angina. The little poof of a coward probably fled back to the lodge.

Screw him. I'll pick him off later, along with that runner.

As a last thought, he slid his left hand beneath his fancy-stitched suit and brought out the pill bottle. He spilled the pills out in a lazy line upon the dusty trail, letting his hand and the vial rest next to them.

Nice touch, he thought, gripping the gun in his other hand as he slitted his eyes to wait.

After what seemed a very long time, he saw Maggie, leading the horse and its cargo, stop ten feet away from him.

"Mr. Carlisle?" she called. "Mr. Carlisle, are you all right? Have you had another attack?"

Stupid wench. He groaned a little, his fingers tightening on the pistol's grip. Got to get her closer. Make it a clean shot. His eyes weren't what they used to be.

She took a step toward him, then stopped. The body on the horse was Gus's, all right. Same chaps, same boots. Same hat. Finally, something had gone right. And in a moment, he'd add one to his body count for the day.

"Mr. Carlisle?" she said again. "Rance?"

How sweet. She was using his Christian name. He supposed he didn't *have* to kill her right away. Nobody else was out here. Grady and Mercury were probably both hiding back at the lodge, like rabbits shivering in their hutches on market day.

He almost smiled, then caught himself. He made his mouth work twice, as if he were attempting to talk but couldn't, and then he said, "M-miss Maguire?" and allowed himself to flutter his eyes open. He'd have to be careful with her. She'd been trouble before. She was likely trouble all the time, from what he'd learned from her background check. But she was only a woman, after all. Just how much trouble could she be?

"Dear Mr. Carlisle!" Maggie said, her face all innocence

and worry. Oh, she was ripe! "Would you like some water? Would it help, Rance?"

He nodded weakly and whispered, "Water." He'd get her to come over and bend down, and then he'd have a sudden "recovery" and roll her over. Pin her to the ground. He'd get a knee between her legs, then—

"Sorry," she said, in a totally different tone of voice. Suddenly hard, suddenly all business. "We're fresh out of that and whatever else it was that you wanted. You don't hide your facial features all that well, Sam."

"S-sam?" he whispered, and cursed himself for whatever tic or minute gesture had given him away. He could still save it, though. He wouldn't get to take her, but he could fix it. "D-don't understand," he said, and eased the gun halfway out of his pocket. "Pills. Need my . . . pills."

She stood over him and back a few feet, at the horse's head, her arms crossed. "Time to stop pretending, Mr. Warden. As they say on the Barbary Coast, the jig's up."

No, he couldn't fix it. But he could fix her. Slowly, he pulled himself up into a sitting position. He wouldn't be able to reach the Winchester from here, but his handgun was on his far side, now drawn free of his pocket. He held it low, behind his back. All pretenses were gone, now. He said, "How did you know?"

She shrugged. "Little things. For instance, that you knew how to work the Edison."

"Anybody could have—"

"No," she broke in. "Hardly anyone. They're new, so new they've barely reached the marketplace. So new that Grady had to pull all kinds of strings to get his. But you knew how to work it. Remember that first night, when you said, 'Just crank the damn thing'?"

He scowled. Stupid remark! He tried to save it by saying, quickly, "I've got one at the ranch. I'm a rich man, you know."

"Oh, that's right," said Maggie. "A rich cattle rancher who doesn't know tenderloin from chuck. That same night, the last of the beef was a chuck roast. But I specifically remember you calling it tenderloin. Shame on you, Mr. Warden, slipping up on a thing like that."

"Well, anyone could have made that mistake!" he roared. Quickly, he calmed himself and added, "I was upset. We were all upset. Being left like that. It was a disgrace." He'd best do it quickly. He began to ease his hand forward.

"And then there were the pills." Didn't she ever shut up? "Sugar. Simple sugar." She clucked her tongue and shook her head.

That did it. There was only so much a man could take. In a blur, he brought the gun up from his side and fired. And hit air. The horse had spooked and she'd vaulted to the side, and he'd had barely time to take that in when the corpse leapt from the skittering horse and he felt fire in his hand.

A glance down showed him he'd been shot through the knuckle, the gun was blown free and his index finger was hanging by a shred of skin. Roaring, he clambered to his feet and charged Gus, head down to ram him.

But Gus's gun barked again, this time catching him in the shoulder. He fell to the side grabbing at his coat and thinking that Sam Warden didn't get shot, by Christ, and sure as hell didn't get shot by a dead man! He reached out with his good hand to grab Gus's legs, to knock them out from under him, to finish him off for good and all with his bare hands.

"Enough!" called Maggie, from behind him.

He heard a *click* as a gun's hammer was cocked. He froze.

"You bitch," Warden snarled, staring at the ground, holding his shoulder.

"Now, now," said Gus. Not Gus. Not Gus's voice. "Let's not bandy names about, shall we?"

He looked up. Grady Maguire. The four-eyed sonofabitch had put on Gus's clothes and played possum. "Damn you," he growled.

"And let's keep the language to a minimum, old man," Grady continued, lowering his pistol. "Ladies present and all that. Now, what do you say you climb up on your feet?"

Those years in prison flashed through his mind. Dark, dank, everything molding and dripping water, the stench of the inmates, and of himself. He wasn't going back.

He'd taken down most of them, though, by God. His "A" list, his most hated enemies. And he'd take one more before he went down.

"But I'm shot!" he said pathetically, and opened his coat with his bloody hand as if to examine the wound more carefully. Funny, it didn't hurt at all.

"Grady, don't let him—" he heard Maggie say as he pulled the derringer secreted in the holster under his arm. The gun was suddenly in both his hands, and aimed straight at Grady's head.

At the same instant he squeezed the trigger, Grady ducked and threw himself to the side, into the clear. And less than half a heartbeat after he fired, while he was shifting the gun to aim it at Grady again, there came another shot from behind him.

Warden twisted toward it, his derringer falling from his hand. He felt no pain. There was only a sense of numbness and of surprise at seeing the smoking pistol in Maggie's hand. And then sudden cold, and then nothing.

Grady, still crouching, tore his gaze away from the body and looked at Maggie. "Is he dead?"

Maggie kicked Warden's discarded pistol to the side, then picked it up and dropped it in her pocket. "Oh, suds," she said. "I think so." She stood up, and with a dusty shoe nudged the derringer out of Warden's fingers. She picked that up, too. "He didn't give me much of a chance to wing him, falling backward like that. I thought you said you frisked him."

Grady colored. "Well, I did! He must've had it, well, I don't know!"

Dust billowed as she pounded at her skirts, mumbling, "Dark green! Why did I have to wear dark green today?" Then louder, "Well, help me drag him up on the horse."

Grady grimaced. "Mags, I'm not moving too well, myself."

She bent to Warden's body, feeling his neck for a pulse. "He didn't shoot you, did he?" Apparently she couldn't find a pulse through all the fat, and picked up his wrist instead. She dropped to her knees and pressed her head to his chest. "Wait," she said. "I can't believe it. He's breathing! Heart's steady."

"Oh, goody. And nobody shot me, by the way," said Grady, a little offended. "As if you'd care." He didn't see her listening to *his* chest.

Carefully, she rolled Warden over and felt his back. "He'll live. Hit a rib." From her voice, he couldn't tell if she was proud or disappointed. She stood up. "Well, he can travel by horse. Do you want to help me—Grady?" she said. "What's wrong?"

Well, she'd noticed he was alive, anyway. Crossing his arms indignantly, he said, "For starters, I've been all over this island today. I've cut down a cat, cut you down, hiked back to the lodge, found another body, then barely had any lunch at all when Gus's horse came galloping in and I had to start hiking all over again. It's hotter than Hades out here, and Gus's boots are too small. And his pants are too tight. It's not three in the afternoon yet, and I think I have permanent internal damage from being slung over this appalling beast for six miles." The horse snorted, and he made a face at it.

"Oh, Grady," she said, in that condescending schoolmarm tone that drove him crazy. "Only a mile and a half, if that." She tipped her head, her brow furrowing. "You do look a little green, though."

"Green? I feel positively chartreuse! And to add insult

to injury, I . . . well, I ripped my britches. Gus's britches. There at the end, when I ducked."

Maggie's hand covered her mouth, but he could tell she was laughing. "Oh, I'm sure you find it very funny," he said, annoyed and just a little more humiliated than he'd care to admit. "After all, *your* britches are still in one piece. And where in thunder are Gus and Mercury?"

From the ground, Warden groaned.

"Hand me the rope," Maggie said, kneeling to Warden. Grady threw it to her. He wasn't getting one step closer to Carlisle—Warden—until the brute was immobilized. Actually, he was rather disappointed that the man was still breathing. No, make that *very* disappointed. Not that he'd wish a dog or cat dead—hell, not even a goldfish!—but he didn't believe Warden had demonstrated that he was quite that high up on the evolutionary scale.

Frankly, he would have been just as happy if she'd blown Warden's head off. Happier still if she'd blasted the pieces of it into the next county, or at least out to sea. And he was still feeling guilty about that derringer. How in the devil could he have missed it? How stupidly amateurish of him!

At least Maggie hadn't mentioned it again, but he'd be kicking himself for a very long time.

Tying Warden's hands before him, Maggie glanced up at Grady and added, "You know, I'd forgotten all about Mercury and Gus. I really thought they'd be here by now. They were supposed to—"

"Here we are!" Gus called hoarsely from the weeds. A moment of crackling sounds later, he emerged, half-dragging Mercury.

"What happened?" asked Maggie, still kneeling.

"Well, these boots'a Grady's is too big and it's hard to walk. And then Mercury, here, peeked under his bandage and passed out on me again. Dangedest thing I ever seen. A body'd think—"

"I can't help it," Mercury said, as Gus leaned him

against a tree. Mercury slithered down it and landed on his seat with a *plop*. "It's the sight of blood. My own anyway. I was fine until he started talking about how badly he'd shot me. A fine thing, bragging to your victim!" Just then, he seemed to notice the body. He swallowed hard. "Is he dead?"

"No," quipped Grady. "More's the pity."

Maggie was looking at Warden's index finger, which was still bleeding heavily. Grady asked, "Maggie, do you need some rags? I believe these pants I'm wearing would do."

"What'd you do to my britches?" cried Gus, bending down. "Aw Christ, he's gone and split 'em!"

"Just a kerchief will do," said Maggie, without looking up. She shook her head. "Did you do this on purpose? And hand down your penknife."

"Kn-knife?" said Mercury, as Grady handed the kerchief and knife to her.

Maggie opened the blade. "Oh," she said matter-of-factly, "I'm just going to cut off his finger."

Mercury fainted again before she sliced the wisp of skin that tenuously held Warden's finger.

TWENTY-EIGHT

AFTER TWO DAYS OF QUESTIONS AND MOVING BODIES around and more questions and transcriptions and signing affidavits, it had been good to finally settle herself into a seat on a southbound train and open a good book. Now, with Grady dozing in the seat beside her, they were nearing San Francisco and home.

She let the book fall closed in her lap, and sighed. Home. Ozymandias purring in her ear. Otto, with all his elaborate inventions. And Quincy.

She smiled, and felt heat flooding her cheeks at the thought of him—and then another surge as she thought of that good-looking salt, Captain Billings. On the day that he docked and discovered the carnage, he was the one who had stood high on the rocks and shot thc shark. And later, after he and his men had hauled all the bodies up out of the cellar and down the stairs and finally to the boat, he'd asked her if she'd like to have dinner in town, seeing as how she'd been through such an ordeal and all.

Well, she couldn't say no to such a generous invitation, now could she?

She hadn't told Grady, though. She'd said she was going down to the sheriff's office again. Wouldn't do at all to have him lord it over her—or tell Quincy. After all, a girl has her fantasies, too!

Except that Captain Billings—Edgar—had turned out to

be a distinctly unromantic type, and looked quite a bit different once he was out of his sweet little white uniform. Mostly, he wanted all the gory details of the last few days. It seemed he'd made a deal with some newspaper or other.

Maggie turned to look out the window, at the dusk-shadowed scenery rushing by. Well, she'd just decided to remember Captain Billings on the boat in his white shorts instead of in that restaurant, with the remains of her chicken potpie dripping from his hair. No, Quincy liked her for herself. He was always there, waiting, and at moments like these, that was what counted. Good old Quincy.

Grady made a half-snore that came out as a soft, funny snort, and shifted in his seat. At least he'd gotten in his tennis game, even if he'd had to condescend to playing it with her, and even if she'd had to browbeat Gus into guarding Sam Warden for an extra two hours.

Tennis came quite naturally to her (as did most physical sports, once the rules were explained), and it had taken every ounce of self-control she had not to beat him. But she held back, and Grady had been cocky all the rest of the morning. He'd practically forgotten about not finding Warden's derringer.

She pursed her lips, debating again whether to tell him that along with three very long, deep cat scratches she'd discovered on his forearm—good Albatross!—she'd found grass inside Warden's well-concealed shoulder rig while she was cleaning up his wounds back at the lodge. Doubtless he'd hidden the derringer back in the brush, where he'd hidden the pistol—and the rifle they'd found later—when he had heard Grady coming up the path.

No. She wouldn't tell him, not yet. Let him suffer a little while longer. Served him right for being such a baby about the whole trip. Well, she supposed she shouldn't be thinking that. It had turned out so badly! But how was she to know that Lolo hadn't really sent the tickets, that the trip wasn't just exactly what it . . .

Damn. She was doing it again, and she'd promised herself she wouldn't. It couldn't have been helped, that was all there was to it. And if she and Grady hadn't gone, there likely would have been six deaths instead of four. No, seven. He couldn't have let Mrs. Friar live, could he? No witnesses.

She shuddered involuntarily.

It was dark outside, now, and they were just coming to the outskirts of the city. How lovely to go home and fall into a chair and get some rest for a change!

She reached over and shook Grady's arm gently. "We're almost home, Grady. Grady? Are you awake?"

Groggily, he opened one eye. "Certainly. No cream."

She grinned and shook him a little more firmly. "Grady, I'm waking you up, not asking how you want your coffee."

He came all the way awake this time and said, rather indignantly, "Well, of course. Who in the world mentioned coffee?" Then he blinked a few times and glanced out the window. "San Francisco?"

"Yes, dear," she said, like a mother with an interminably cute child. "You wired Otto, didn't you?"

"Yes, Mags," he replied in the same tone as he rose to bring their hand luggage down from the overhead.

"I really should write Lolo," she said, more to herself than Grady.

"Yes, you should," he said, handing her a frayed carpetbag. "You should figure out a code or something, in case this ever happens again. So you'll know it's really her, and not some maniacal killer out to slaughter us in our beds and bathrooms."

She grinned as he pulled down his hand luggage and sat down, clearing the aisle just in time for the conductor, who walked down the aisle calling, "San Francisco! Next stop San Francisco!"

"Grady?" she said, as she tucked her novel inside the carpetbag. Maybe two days of withholding was enough. Perhaps she should tell him.

He wasn't listening, though. "Mags," he said, staring

past her at the city lights rushing toward them, "I just can't figure how I missed . . . Well, I can't believe I missed that pocket gun." He held up his hands and stared at them like traitors. "I can't puzzle it out. Let alone that pistol. Well, he must have tossed it in the grass or something. But he would have kept the little gun on him, wouldn't he? In case I caught on to him? Or even in case I didn't? After all those years of picking pockets, you'd think that—"

Maggie couldn't stand it anymore. "Grady?"

"I mean, really! I could see missing a dried pea, but something so big as a pocket gun is—"

"Grady?"

"—absolutely absurd. I should be hauled out in the streets and publicly horsewhipped by the pickpockets' union, if we had one, or . . . Did you say something?"

"Yes, Grady. You didn't miss it."

He pulled himself up. "Well, of course, I did. He had it on him, didn't he? All tucked away in some little well padded hidey-hole under his shirt. That's the only thing I can think of. Padding. Of course, it would have to be specially made, and . . ."

Maggie missed the rest of this diatribe, for just then the train pulled into the station, and the noise of brakes and steel on steel and jetting steam drowned out all else for a few moments. Grady's mouth, she noticed with a silent smile, just kept on moving.

Otto was waiting on the platform to greet them and the normally undemonstrative Maggie threw her arms around him and hugged him so hard that the old toymaker yelped.

"Sorry, Otto," she said sheepishly, and threaded her arm through his. It was just that she was so glad to see his broad, muttonchops face again. To see anyone's face, for that matter! She'd only begun to realize these past few days how close she'd come to never seeing anyone again.

"Is hinky-dinky," Otto replied. "No bones do you break." He seemed a little off-balance—probably thrown there by her overly enthusiastic greeting.

Scouting down the line for Grady, who was collecting the luggage, she said, "How's Ozzie? And Quincy?" She spied Grady then, helping a porter load their mismatched bags.

"Both hinky-dinky. On the telephone, your Quincy calls. He says to say he has a big meeting tonight, but tomorrow you maybe go to dinner with him at some fancy-schmantzy place. I forget where." He rubbed his shoulder. "You going to tell an old man what happens, *liebchen*? Too happy you are to be seeing me."

Maggie laughed, and Otto screwed his face into one of those disapproving grimaces, which made her laugh all the harder. Lord, it was great to be alive!

As she pulled Otto down the line toward Grady, she was still grinning like a fool. "I'll tell you at dinner, Otto," she said. "We'll both tell you."